Also by Maggie Sims

The School of Enlightenment Series

Roslynn's Rebellion (prequel novella)
Sophia's Schooling (Book 1)
Penelope's Passion (Book 2)
Althea's Awakening (Book 3)
Beth's Behavior (Book 4)

Spin-off

Ann's Angel (a Christmas short story)

The Control Series

Charlotte's Control (Book 1)
Lyon's Lover (Book 2)

Even at an all-girls school in Regency England, workplace romances can prove challenging

Regina shuddered, afraid to let her hope free. Her previous thought was wrong. A simple look was not enough to risk her future. She needed a clear declaration of interest.

Helen had levered up on her elbows and twisted around to look at her.

"Regina." Her voice was lower, with gravel in it.

"Helen. What do you want?"

"I want…" Helen took a deep breath. "I want you."

Regina's core flooded at the words, but she had to be sure. This school taught an enlightened approach to intimacy, but as far as she knew, Helen had only ever been interested in men.

"Do you mean a massage?"

"If that is what you are comfortable with. I am interested in more caresses than a massage involves, but only if it suits you." Helen was blushing but held her gaze.

"What about"—her hand flipped over and back again on Helen's arse—"your husband?"

"He's dead these past few years, dear." Helen grinned at her.

PRAISE FOR

Maggie Sims

"Sexy, witty, emotionally rich writing and incredible **heat** make Maggie Sims a must read! She leaves readers—and her characters—desperate for more! Fierce, fearless heroines are her specialty!"

~ *Tracy Sumner, USA Today Bestselling Author of* The Duchess Society *series*

~*~

"In *Sophia's Schooling*, Maggie Sims strikes a perfect balance of proper manners and delicious perversity. Her characters are deftly sketched, and the flavors of sex and punishment are sure to excite even the most discerning of kinky-historical readers."

~ *Annabel Joseph, NYT and USA Today bestselling author of* The Properly Spanked *series*

~*~

"*Penelope's Passion* is…a wonderful story of forbidden romance from two people in very different life circumstances just trying to do the right thing for both themselves and their families…readers who like an extra spicy historical romance will not want to miss out!"

~ *Golden Angel, USA Today Bestselling Authorof the* Bridal Discipline *series*

Helen's House

by

Maggie Sims

A School of Enlightenment Spinoff

This is a work of fiction. Names, characters, places, and incidents are either the product of the author's imagination or are used fictitiously, and any resemblance to actual persons living or dead, business establishments, events, or locales, is entirely coincidental.

Helen's House

Cover by *Lisa Dawn MacDonald*

Publishing History
First Edition, 2024
Trade Paperback ISBN 979-8-89044-403-5
Digital ISBN 979-8-89044-404-2

Chapter One

Spring 1818, Hertfordshire

Regina Carlisle held back a moan behind gritted teeth as she dropped her booted foot to the ground with a thump.

"Daggers," she hissed under her breath as pain shot up her back. She glanced at Cecilia, the student who was assisting her effort to achieve the saddle, hoping she hadn't heard the curse.

Cecilia stepped back. "I'm sorry, Mistress. I need to get to my late class. Perhaps we can try again tomorrow?"

"Ta, Cecilia. Enjoy your learning." Regina had no doubt the girl would. Cecilia was one of many eager pupils at the School of Enlightenment. She'd arrived a fresh-faced innocent and would leave in less than a month just as bright-eyed but much less innocent, having learned the tools of managing her life and happiness at the secret finishing academy.

Regina, meanwhile, needed to find a way to exercise her babies. Each horse might weigh seventy-five stone, but they were still her babies. Her role as stablemistress for the school was everything she'd dreamed of in a post, or in her life, for that matter. She was determined to do it well and avoid risking her future here.

If only she had not slipped on a patch of ice three days ago and injured herself. This snowfall had been a

March surprise, coming after a day of rain which had frozen under the snow. It made clearing the path from the main building to the stables quite a strenuous job and by the end of it, she'd tired and gone down hard on her bottom. At thirty-three, she had a well-cushioned posterior but was slower to recover, and the injury prevented her from lifting her leg over the saddle.

Even so, she had zero regrets about not learning to ride sidesaddle, which might be feasible with her sore muscles. But sidesaddle was the way to a broken neck, far worse than a bruised bottom. Growing up she'd always preferred breeches or trousers to dresses and skirts. These days, she wore a split skirt, or what she thought of as wide-legged trousers, and encouraged all staff and students to do the same for riding.

She sighed. She'd need to request help if she was unable to ride in the morning. Not wanting to draw attention to herself was unfair to the horses. They'd gotten no exercise for days with the inclement weather keeping other riders indoors.

She ducked into her rooms at the rear of the stables, beyond the tack room, to rest her back before attempting to forage for food. Usually, she ventured to the dining hall in the main building in hopes of seeing her secret crush. The odds of her seeing the lush, enticing form of the headmistress, much less speaking to her, were slim, but as her eyes closed, she could not resist conjuring Helen Montague's fair form.

That arse, those breasts, her warm eyes and inviting lips. Imagining her caused a spurt of warmth in Regina's stomach, but imagining was all she allowed herself. Tonight, she'd make do with the snacks and scraps she had in her room rather than attempt that trek with a sore back.

The headmistress's assistant, Grace, would be in bright and early in the morning. Regina would speak to her then. She'd prefer to avoid encountering the lovely headmistress and jeopardizing the role she loved so much. Grace would find someone to assist Regina for a day or two, and Helen never needed to know.

* * * *

Helen Montague leaned back in her office chair and stretched her arms overhead. She blinked a few times, realizing how dim the room was. She'd pulled the oil lamp so close to her as she worked, she hadn't even noticed the day coming to an end. Thankfully, the window was cracked despite the cold temperatures, given how much soot the light generated. She was eager for spring's longer days. They would bring better light to work by, but perhaps more importantly, provide an opportunity to enjoy the sun on her face and alleviate her post-winter ghostlike pallor.

Knocks thumped on her door, and she glanced up at the open crack. Given the time, her assistant Grace would likely have gone to supper.

"Come in," she called.

A Scottish student with brown skin, dark hair, and a ready smile entered. She was a favorite with the staff due to her positive attitude. Having completed the introductory course, she was in her final weeks of the advanced course.

"Good evening, Cecilia. I'm surprised you are not at supper. How are classes going?"

"Quite well, thank you, Mrs. Montague. I'm sorry

to disturb you."

"Nonsense. I am always available to you and happy to help." She smiled. "Would you like to sit?"

"No, thank you. I'm on my way to supper and don't wish to disturb the other diners by being tardy. But…" She wrung her hands.

"What is amiss?" Helen's brows creased with worry.

"It may not be my place to say…" Cecilia took a deep breath. "But I'm worried about Mistress Regina."

"Oh?" Confusion layered on Helen's worry. "Perhaps you'd best explain. What is wrong?" she repeated.

"She hurt her back the day after the snow and has not yet been able to ride. No one else has been riding, either, given the cold and the mud as the snow melted. The horses are getting restless. And, er, so is Mistress Regina. I was wondering if you minded if a few of us took an afternoon away from class to help her?"

"Oh no. Do I need to call a physician?"

"Uh…" Cecilia grimaced.

"I beg your pardon, Cecilia. Of course, you are not in a position to know that. I shall check on the stablemistress myself. After I speak to her, we can determine next steps. I appreciate you bringing this to my attention and your generous offer to help."

"You'll let me know? The beasties"—Helen smiled at the common Scottish vernacular from Cecilia's childhood—"want to enjoy the spring like the rest of us. And I worry about Mistress Regina trying to do too much."

"I shall find you tomorrow. I promise," Helen vowed.

As Cecilia left for supper, Helen stood. Then groaned. Lud, she was stiff from hunching over the never-ending pile of paperwork that running the school entailed. There were letters to the founders, progress reports to the sponsors, authorization of recruiting efforts from her helpers around the country, as well as reviewing financial records, approving new curriculum requests, and hiring.

The school had only begun a few years before to equip young women with the knowledge to manage their own futures and sexualities, founded by a group led by the generous Lady Roslynn and her reluctant-at-first husband, Lord Suffolk. By the end of the first year, they'd barely been able to keep up with the demand for placements. Given the secret nature of the institution, the founders, including Helen, had expected to have to tiptoe through the gossip mill that was the Ton, handpicking potential students and sponsors with extreme caution. And they had—and continued to do so—but it was amazing what a few well-placed comments by the right aristocrats could cultivate. Particularly when said lords belonged to a spanking club that prided itself on its vetting of members and privacy.

Helen shook her head. When the London-based founders had approached her about the idea, she'd been impressed with their vision. She'd offered the land she'd inherited at her husband's passing and to head the school temporarily. While unsure if she was the right person for the role given her sheltered life, she nonetheless had the time and resources to help.

Instead, it had become her passion. Four years in, however, she was struggling to keep up with the pace of growth. She'd enjoyed the tasks required to set up the school, especially finding the teachers and students. Now, she would love to hand off the daily administration of running the buildings, staff, and grounds, if she only had time to hire someone.

Her lips twisted in self-recrimination. She'd been trying to find a new staff member for more than two months but had not been able to give it her full attention with the many urgent tasks that arose daily.

As she maneuvered out of her office and paced toward the stables, she evaluated her stiffness and the fact that her clothes were growing ever tighter. Despite the never-ending amount of work that required her attention, she should exercise a bit more. She used to walk or ride almost daily, but she'd let the days get away from her these past months. Regina's injury was well-timed, if unfortunate. 'Twas the perfect excuse to get some fresh air.

* * * *

Helen knocked on the door to Regina's room. She heard movement then a groan. Concerned, she did not wait for an invitation. She swung the door open to peer in, hoping she would not find the stablemistress on the floor. Given how stiff she was, she wasn't sure she could lift the taller woman.

Dark eyes, wide with surprise, stared at her. "Helen," Regina gasped, perched gingerly on the edge of the bed.

"How are you, Regina?" Helen bustled over and peered at her, looking for signs of pain.

"I am getting better. Let me guess, Cecilia was concerned about 'the beasties?'"

"She was worried about you. As am I." Helen could see the pinches around Regina's eyes and mouth in an otherwise stoic countenance. She wanted to pat Regina in reassurance, but they'd never had the type of relationship that allowed for casual touches.

"She's a sweet girl. I would have come to find you or Grace tomorrow if I could not ride. The girls"—Regina gestured toward the door Helen had entered through—"should not suffer for my injury."

"Shall we have the physician from town out tomorrow?" For the quiet, independent stablemistress to consider asking for help meant the pain must be severe.

Regina shook her head. "I'm relatively certain 'tis a pulled muscle." She explained the ice under the snow.

"You poor dear. What if 'tis something worse, though?"

"It has improved each day, hence my expert diagnosis." Regina offered a self-deprecating, one-sided grin.

Helen returned her smile. She'd give it one more day to see for herself before making the decision to call in a physician. Changing the subject, she said, "D'you know, Cecilia offered to gather a few friends to take the girls out tomorrow?"

"Like I said, sweet. But I hope to be well enough to do it myself by then. And with today having been warmer, perhaps some students or staff with free time will want to ride." Regina echoed Helen's preferences on interfering with students' learning.

Cecilia's classes in the advanced course offered less free time than the introductory course. Girls new to the school needed time to assimilate to the independence and learning offered them. And some students were proficient in the foundational subjects, so they had use of the grounds during those classes.

"Very well. I shall check with you in the morning. If nothing else, I plan to help." She half-turned toward the door.

"Nnnooo."

Helen frowned, tucking her chin in confusion at the vehement tone.

Regina cleared her throat and adjusted her response. "I beg your pardon. I am grateful for the offer, but you have the entire school to run. I'm certain Grace and I can find a few people to step in, even if we call on townspeople."

"And how will you do that, if you can't ride?" She put her hands on her hips.

"Er, Grace?"

Dropping her hands, Helen shook her head. "It will take less time away from managing the school if I help. Her workload is as heavy as mine."

"Oh." Regina seemed at a loss.

"Now that we've settled the matter, how can I serve you this evening?" Helen edged closer, smiling to put the other woman at ease. It was easy to take charge after running the school these past years, and she truly was happy to help.

Regina's brows rose. "Helen. You've just said you are very busy. You've offered to assist tomorrow. I do not mean to sound ungrateful, but I hate the idea of taking more of your time than necessary. I do not need a nurse. This, too, shall pass."

"Nonsense. I can't see to read or write anyway. 'Tis dark. Have you eaten?"

Flattening her lips, Regina stared at her.

"No? I haven't either. I shall go get us a picnic from the kitchen and bring it back here. Don't run off, now." She giggled at her silly attempt at a joke.

Regina continued to stare. Perhaps Helen's attempt at humor had been weak, but it was clear that Regina needed sustenance. As did she.

She hurried to the main building and grabbed a variety of offerings for a cold supper. Walking back, her arms laden with bread and cold meats, a carafe of wine tucked under one arm, a memory rose in her mind.

George, her husband for nearly twenty years before his death, had wrenched his back doing fence work on their land and been in agony for days. They'd tried hot and cold compresses but nothing had eased the pain. She'd been helping in the stables in his place when she spied their stable hand rubbing a horse down with camphor oil. Snatching it up as soon as he finished, she returned to her bed-ridden husband and rubbed his back with the oil.

He'd asked her to dig into the muscles with her thumbs and fists, moaning in relief when she did. He'd been up and walking the next day, although he did not lift anything heavy for a few more days.

Regina was one of the quietest, most caring people she knew, and from their few prior conversations, it was clear the stablemistress was as passionate about the school as she was. Regardless, the woman was in pain, and she was Helen's responsibility, like the rest of the staff. She'd explain the idea, and hopefully Regina would overcome any shyness about baring her lower back. They were both women, after all. What was a little touch between coworkers if it helped speed her recovery?

As she bustled in with her food offerings, she saw that Regina had moved a few things around. The room had already been neat, even sparse. Now, the tiny table and two wooden chairs had been pulled out of the corner and plates were set out. There were large checkered handkerchiefs folded as napkins. Helen placed the food on the table and sat down across from Regina. The stablemistress had removed the tie from her dark hair, and it fell forward to frame her face. While Helen's own hair was turning gray, they were closer in age than much of the staff. Once the stablemistress was back to full strength, a friendship could be forged if Helen made the time.

Over supper, she asked Regina about the amount of exercise each horse needed and on any other chores she'd struggled with the past few days.

The other woman balked at further assistance. "I've been hurt worse falling off a recalcitrant horse."

Helen narrowed her eyes at Regina, dissecting the response. The school ensured the mares were docile for all levels of riders. Which meant Regina's fall had been when she was several years younger and more resilient. Distracted by worries of how to bring up the idea of a rubdown, she let the comment pass. She poured them each a second glass of wine, exhaling a tired sigh as she propped herself against the chair back.

"If I may ask, what did you do before the school was founded?" Regina asked.

Helen circled the glass of wine in a negligent gesture. "I was a working farmer's wife on this land. I cared for the yard animals and the house; George took care of the barn and beyond. Without all the staff we have now, it took every waking moment."

"Did you enjoy it?"

"I did…" Helen chose her next words carefully. "At the time. I could not return to it now. My husband was a lovely man, a decade my senior and, of course, the ruler of our household. I was not aware of any other choices. Now, I love being surrounded by smart, forward-thinking women, making my own decisions, and having my own career."

"Was running a school a difficult transition?"

"Surprisingly, no."

Regina tilted her head in question, her hair blending with the serviceable dark brown of her dress.

"When I started, I thought it was temporary. I'd get the school set up and hand it off, and build a little cottage for myself in a private nook out there." She gestured. "But seeing young women come in as girls and leave ready to take on the world was addicting. I wanted to bring more in, and offer them a wider set of options, and ensure they had room and space to grow without men in the way."

Regina laughed.

Helen poured out the rest of the carafe, surprised at how quickly they'd finished it. Regina was easy to talk to, which surprised her given how little the stablemistress socialized. When Regina raised her brows at the wineglasses Helen muttered, "It will help you sleep." At speaking volume, she continued. "I never liked Town. I've always preferred the country with less rules. This is a way to offer girls that experience, even if they have to return to London. They can take that feeling of freedom with them and find ways to insert it into their lives, whether they are Ton or working for the Ton, or whatever. 'Tis the same reason I could not go back to a traditional marriage."

Helen's cheeks felt hot. She could not remember the last time she'd had three glasses of wine or talked so much. Then again, nor could she recall the last time she'd offered to rub camphor into a coworker's back muscles. A little liquid courage was needed here.

"You know, my husband used to get lower back cramps when he overdid it." She gulped as Regina's shocked gaze snapped up to meet hers, and her next words were rushed through tight lips. "If I rubbed camphor oil on it and kneaded the muscle, it helped."

Chapter Two

The knock had surprised Regina as she lay in bed and let her mind drift. When her employer opened the door before she could stand, Regina thought she'd conjured her.

No, I would have evoked her naked.

Then Helen had insisted on bringing her food and eating with her. And questioning her on what needed doing. When the headmistress filled their wineglasses a third time, Regina shot her a surprised glance. Helen was flushed, and Regina suspected that with the demands of her work, the headmistress did not indulge in three glasses of wine too often. Nor did she, and she could feel her blood rush and her body heat. Or was that simply Helen's proximity?

When the headmistress fumbled out a comment about rubbing oil into her husband's skin, Regina could only stare silently, mouth agape. Was she offering what Regina thought she might be? She'd like nothing better than this woman's hands on her body, but she needed to be certain she understood correctly.

The other woman was staring at her empty plate and fidgeting with her silverware.

Ready to sit up and beg, Regina nonetheless remained silent.

"I would be happy to do the same for you..." Helen said to her plate.

Yes, please!

No, Helen was clearly uncomfortable with the idea. Also, Regina was not sure she could be responsible for her actions, employment or no, if Helen caressed any part of her. She'd yearned for Helen since meeting her, but she'd also dreamed of a place of work like this one, safe among open-minded people and away from the world's condemnation of her dress, her height…her preferences in lovers.

She gulped. "'Tis a lovely gesture, ta, Helen. But not necessary. I shall be fine."

Helen stood and strode out to the stables, without so much as a farewell.

Regina tilted her head at the odd behavior, but within a minute Helen was back with camphor oil from the tack room.

Regina leaned back a little, her eyes widening.

"Nonsense. We are both women, our bodies are the same—well, other than mine being older and heavier." She smiled at Regina.

Regina blinked. Helen's shyness of moments before was gone. In the face of indecision—apparently, even her own—Helen was always the one to step in and take charge. Regina hadn't thought much about their ages, but apparently Helen had. She wanted to reassure the headmistress that her curves were beautiful and lush, the gray streaks in her blonde hair a sign of maturity and responsibility, but she daren't.

"Come now. Why don't you change into your nightclothes? Have you a wrapper?" Helen glanced around. Her voice was high, her speech fast.

She's still nervous. But so determined. Regina moved one shoulder in a lopsided shrug. Who was she to interfere with Helen's decisions, or to miss an opportunity like this. If nothing else, it would provide self-pleasure fantasies for ages. Thank goodness she had something to cover herself. She did not own any nightrails, as she slept naked.

Helen moved to clean up the remains of their meal, giving her a modicum of privacy.

Regina shucked her dress, worn stays that provided gentle support without being restrictive, and camisole, and threw on her wrapper. As she bent to lie on the bed, an unintended groan slipped out.

Helen whirled around. "Let me help you," she said, rushing to Regina's side.

"I'm there." She'd managed to stretch out face down and sighed in relief when the prone position rewarded her with fewer twinges of pain. Turning her head against the pillow, she watched Helen grab the vial.

She stood hovering by the bed, biting her lip, her fingers white around the oil.

Regina searched for a way to allay her boss's nerves, but came up blank.

"Er, you said lower back?" The headmistress's eyes were narrowed, flicking from her shoulder to her calf where the hem of the wrapper lay.

Regina realized Helen wasn't sure how to bare the area and still offer her some modesty. She held back a snort of laughter. If only she could strip off the robe and entice her lovely employer. She was not shy. But sadly, her figure was quite different than George's and therefore unlikely to tempt Helen.

With careful movements, she shrugged one shoulder out of the wrapper, then her arm. "Does this work? You can peel it back to where you need it."

"Oh, yes. Thank you." Helen tugged the muslin down to Regina's waist.

"You can sit. Or kneel. There's no need to injure your back too, leaning over me."

"Right, then." Helen perched on the bed, hip to face-down hip with Regina. Her deep purple skirts spread around her.

The stopper of the vial popped and Regina closed her eyes. An oil-filled hand slid down one side of her spine and she shivered in pleasure.

The hand withdrew. "Did I hurt you?"

"No, 'tis a bit cold," she lied.

Please, put your hand back.

Just that touch had her pulse racing and perspiration breaking out under her arms. She hoped Helen wouldn't feel the pounding of her heart shake the bed.

Regina chastised herself. She needed to stop acting like a silly, untried girl.

Forcing herself back to stillness, she tried to calm her breathing. Helen's hand returned on the other side of her spine.

"Where does it hurt?"

"There and a bit lower." Regina barely stopped herself from snorting at the unintentional innuendo.

"Right. I shall need to pull your robe down a little farther."

Yes, please. Regina gave herself a mental eye-roll at the repeated begging. She needed to stop dreaming. Just because Helen talked about how much the school had opened her eyes to the joys of less traditional relationships did not mean she was suddenly romantically, or even physically, interested in women.

Helen drove her thumbs into the dimples at the top

of Regina's buttocks.

Regina groaned, long and low.

"There?"

"Yes. Yes. My word, that feels wonderful." She would have named several other places she'd prefer Helen's thumbs—her mouth, her breasts, her now-wet sex. But that was before she'd felt the marvel of them unraveling these knotted muscles. Now, she might happily live without orgasms for this relief.

"'Tis very similar to George's ailment. I am going to manipulate the muscles around it as well."

Lower. Definitely lower.

As though she'd voiced her request aloud, Helen's hands moved downward and toward her sides a little, working up in an inverted vee back to the base of her spine.

Regina panted. The removal of pain and addition of sensual desire were potent. Her folds grew more damp, and her breasts swelled against the sheet. She wished Helen to lie alongside her, to finish the rubdown and change her touch to long strokes along her back, her bottom, between her legs for more intimate caresses. On the other hand, she dreamed of reversing their positions, so she could reward this nurturing woman who took care of everyone before herself.

Helen shifted. "My back does not enjoy this twist. If you do not mind…" She rose, turned, and knelt, one knee between Regina's legs, one on the outside where she'd been sitting.

"You won't hurt me if you sit on me." *I might die from ecstasy, but you won't hurt me*.

"I'll sit on my heels, but you might get a bit of my weight. This way, I can rub as well as knead." Helen placed her hands so her thumbs nearly met on Regina's lower back, her fingers on the sides of her waist.

Regina sighed and tried to relax. Her eyes drifted shut again, committing every aspect of this interlude to memory.

Helen's hands inched lower, her thumb pressure firm but no longer digging.

She was nearly cupping Regina's bottom cheeks and it took everything in Regina not to bow up—to beg. Helen's hot center rested on her left thigh, making Regina twitch with the desire to flip over, to touch, to lick. Pinching the skin of one hand with the other where they rested under her head, she reminded herself this was her employer.

Helen's firm touch slid upward slowly, compressing the long muscles on either side of her spine.

Regina's breath caught as fingers grazed her ribs, then the sides of her breasts where they bulged against the bed. Another spurt of heat flared in her belly, liquefying her insides. To have those fingers pluck her pebbled nipples would be paradise.

Helen reversed direction, scaling up and down twice more.

Each time, Regina fought rigidity, afraid Helen would ask her about pain. Afraid she'd blurt out a plea for a more sensual touch.

Finally, Helen ceased her torture, withdrawing her hands after a last gentle pat.

At the sudden absence of touch, Regina jolted out of her daydreams.

"How does your back feel?" Helen asked, kneeling up to allow her to test it.

"My word." Her voice was awed as she twisted

gently. "I am almost ready to run to town." The pain was still present, but it was a shadow of its former self. "You are a miracle worker, Helen. Thank you ever so much."

"I am happy to help." Helen tugged her wrapper up to her shoulder and climbed to standing.

Regina suppressed a shudder of disappointment.

"Right, then. Get a good night's sleep and I'll be out tomorrow morning. I shall bring breakfast for us so you needn't walk up to the dining hall." With that, the headmistress was gone.

Regina fell asleep within minutes, too relaxed to even take herself over to the memory of that warm mound against the back of her thigh.

* * * *

Helen rose early the next morning to leave Grace a note regarding her absence from the office. Eager to see the stablemistress, she told herself she wanted to see how Regina's back fared. But her brain kept thinking of ways to have more conversations with the engaging woman.

Surprised to find her assistant already at her desk, Helen apprised her of her plan to assist Regina in exercising the mares.

"Shall I help today whilst you review some of the letters applying for the additional assistant role?" Grace cocked her head toward a specific pile on Helen's desk.

The school's growth had brought new programs and new students, faster than any of the board members had anticipated. She'd obtained permission from the overseers to hire a second aide, the position she'd been trying to fill.

"Yes. I should work on that, but I promised Regina

I'd bring her breakfast so she could rest and recover, so I'll pop down with that and return. I shall help as needed with rides tomorrow then. I'd dearly love to spend some time out in this spring weather anyway."

Grace hummed, which Helen took as agreement.

After grabbing sweet buns and tea, she navigated the path to the stables. Spotting Regina pouring buckets of water into the trough, she hurriedly set the teapot and basket on a hay bale. Helen shook her head. The woman clearly had no care for her person; she should not be carrying heavy buckets around.

Angry, she strode closer. "What do you think you're doing?"

Regina blinked and dropped the second bucket to her side.

"You should not be carrying those!" Helen did not wait for an answer. "Give me that!"

Regina held out the bucket, relinquishing her grip once Helen grasped the handle. The bucket dropped, splashing both of their skirts.

Lud, that was heavy!

Even if she'd been prepared for its weight, she would not have been able to carry it far. She stared down at it, then up at her stablemistress. "My goodness, how on earth do you lug that around?"

Regina had hunkered down and was using her own skirt to try to dry Helen's.

Helen reached for Regina's arm to tug her upright. That crouch could not be any better for her back than carrying those ridiculously heavy buckets. When her hand slid around the other woman's upper arm, Regina's head snapped back to stare at her. At the same time, Helen registered the muscles under her hand. There was no softness like in her own arms.

Regina held her gaze, unmoving.

For a long moment, Helen too was frozen. Those dark eyes and the surprisingly taut muscles held her in thrall. A flash of Regina's firm back, paler than her arms and face, but as taut as the arm she gripped, came to mind. Her stomach twinged in a way it hadn't in years. She took a steadying breath and licked her lips.

Regina's eyelids dropped to half-mast.

The stablemistress's preference for female lovers was suddenly foremost in Helen's mind. A twist of warmth in her belly shocked her. 'Twas a thrum of attraction. She'd never consciously been sexually drawn to a woman before.

Living at the school, she'd come to value women and her relationships with them more than she ever had in married life. Intelligence and independence were qualities she looked for in every hire.

Staring at Regina's tall, fit form, the puzzle pieces fit together. Those traits combined with physical beauty invoked desire. She simply had not put them together in the context of a relationship with a woman until now when she literally held them in her hands. She hastily dropped Regina's arm and stepped back.

Regina stood, taking her time.

Helen watched her, but Regina did not meet her eyes. She might have been attempting to avoid back pain, but she also could have been taking a moment to gather herself after the strangely intimate moment they'd just experienced. Helen gave herself a mental headshake. She was being fanciful, letting her imagination get away from her. Regina was an employee and excellent at her trade. She would not overstep. If anyone had, it had been

Helen herself.

"I'll get another bucket of water, shall I?" Regina murmured.

"No. Please do not hurt yourself. A man is coming from the village, at least today and tomorrow. Nor should you be bending to worry about a spill I created."

The stablemistress shook her head. "I cannot sit around and watch people work. D'you think their food is any lighter than this?" She grinned at Helen's shocked gape. "These do not feel heavy to me, I assure you. I'm being careful. I am watching where I walk and not turning or bending too quickly. As much as I enjoyed the rubdown—" she choked and turned red "—I do not want to take you from your duties again, nor do I wish to waste your efforts."

Regina's blush fascinated Helen. The stablemistress had her share of awkward moments, but blushing was new. It was so…feminine, when Regina did not make many efforts toward that characteristic. Her thumb and fingers of the hand that had held Regina's arm rubbed against one another. Tempted to reach for her and explore both of their reactions to her touch, Helen stepped back and reminded herself of the school rules. Mumbling her assent, she excused herself and made her way back to her office.

Already behind, she made little progress the rest of the day. Her brain kept returning to Regina's tall form, laid out under her. She should have expected arms that were fit after feeling all the lean muscles in the woman's back. Indeed, even the woman's bottom had been toned and round under Helen's fingers. She called up Regina standing, hair tied back in a simple tail, face tanned a deep honey color from her outdoor work, lush lips slightly parted.

The stables had never required much oversight on her part, as Regina kept them running smoothly. Only the occasional request for new supplies needed approval. The stablemistress's independence and capabilities in her role had always impressed Helen. Now she almost wished more time had been necessary, so she might have gotten to know Regina. Perhaps she'd feel less awkward about these sudden yearnings.

Lud, it's been too long since you've been intimate with anyone other than your hand. Now, you're conjuring interest from your staff. Stop being ridiculous.

It wasn't as though she could simply trot down to the village pub and proposition a man.

Or a woman.

The words slid into her thoughts like Regina's oiled skin had against her hand. She was surprised she hadn't considered it sooner, given where she lived and worked. It simply hadn't occurred to her—until Regina. But now that it had, it wouldn't leave her alone.

She shook her head. The school taught the girls command of their own bodies and sexuality, but promiscuity was not a leadership quality. Besides, she was more interested in sharing a life with someone than sharing a bed for a night or two. Well, most of the time. Today might be the exception.

She stared at the mess on her desk waiting for her attention. A deep sigh escaped. This was her life right now. She needed to focus on hiring another assistant before she and Grace were completely overwhelmed.

She'd been contemplating returning to the stables to check on Regina after the evening meal, but her workload kept her at her desk well into the dark, with a second oil lamp borrowed from Grace's desk to avoid eye strain.

Chapter Three

Heaving her five-foot-seven frame out of bed the next morning, Regina waited for pain to shoot down toward her thigh or up toward her shoulder, but after a few stretches, her back was vastly improved, only a slight twinge when she bent or twisted.

Regina's amazement at her mobility continued throughout the day. Grace took first shift and rode several of the feistier mares Regina had pointed out. As she dismounted, she muttered, "I'll pay for this time away with all the work waiting, but it was a nice change."

"Ta, Grace. Helen said you both have been very busy. I appreciate the help."

The administrator simply nodded and sped away.

Cecilia came bouncing down after lunch, always happy to help. Her eyes twinkling, she said, "Mistress, you look much…straighter."

"Get on with you." Regina swatted at her with the towel she'd been using to wipe down saddles.

"I am verra glad you are feeling better."

"Hmph. Do not think you are forgiven for telling tales to the headmistress. I told you I'd ask for help if I needed it."

"I won't ask for your pardon." The girl's chin jutted out. "The beasties deserve our best, and this school is all about helping one another. Anyway, admit it. 'Twas nice to have some human company besides me around here."

"Ha. Don't you think I would have chosen a different type of work if I had wanted to be around people?"

"Do you not get lonely?" Cecilia asked.

"The babies talk to me, just as I talk to them. And my helpers are generally better-behaved than you." Cecilia snorted and Regina grinned. "I can talk to people in the dining hall, but what do I have in common with teachers and the like?"

The student quickly replied, "Your love of this school and the principles it represents, for one. I'm sure I shall think of others."

Regina shook her head, still smiling.

Cecilia grew serious. "Mistress, you lived in London before, didn't you?" At Regina's nod, she continued. "What is it like? Did you enjoy it?"

Cecilia was destined for the annual courtesan auction at the Earl of Mansfield's theatre in London, and would likely be set up there by her first benefactor.

"Ah…" Regina saw the girl's concern over an unknown future. "Given my aforementioned preference for horses over people, you will not be surprised to hear that I did not enjoy it. But that is not to say you shan't. I am not one for parties, gossip, and the latest fashions. However, I can see you being the belle of the ball." Regina smiled at the student.

"That sounds fun. Are there less pleasurable aspects?"

"The noise, the crowds, the smells." Regina wrinkled her nose, remembering. "Those can be avoided for the most part, but gossip always has two sides. There are winners and losers, and courtesans walk a fine line on the edge of acceptance."

"Would there not be more tolerance in a big city, where people are more sophisticated?"

Regina snorted, and a horse poked her head out of a stall to investigate the noise. "Not in my experience. There is far more acceptance here."

"Choice, then? Do you not want to find someone to love?"

"Ah, the innocence of youth." Regina patted Cecilia's arm. "I prefer the open-mindedness here over the risks of London, even if I have to forego finding a lifelong partner."

"But—"

"These beasties won't exercise themselves. Get on with you." Regina patted her again and smiled to soften her abrupt halt to the conversation.

* * * *

On the second day, she could not feel more than a pinch. She really owed Helen for this.

Perhaps I can pay in orgasms. She snickered then sobered when Helen knocked on her open door.

"You might be a saint, as whatever you did to my back was a miracle." She gestured for Helen to set the breakfast basket and teapot on the table. Admiring Helen's front then back as she passed, Regina's mind flashed back to the feel of that luscious arse and thighs resting on her.

Helen grinned. "I'm so glad I could help. But—and this is an order—I insist that you ease into things." She held up a hand when Regina frowned and opened her mouth to argue. "We shall see how you feel then."

Regina gaped at her as they sat to eat. "Am I allowed

to lead the mares out to the field at least?"

Helen narrowed her eyes. "I suppose." She belied her hesitant words with a grin, the lines around her eyes deepening into creases that proved her good humor was lifelong.

Regina's heart panged at how beautiful her employer was, especially when she smiled. "Why, thank you, milady," she said with a mock curtsy.

Later that day, after she completed the few tasks the headmistress had allowed, she paused outside the stable door. She had a horse in hand and the sun on her face, two of her favorite things in the world.

If only she had that bossy delectable woman in her bed, her life would be perfect.

No, she argued with her fantasy. First, Helen preferred men or she wouldn't have been married for twenty years. And second, this lovely lady was her employer. Even if Regina seduced her, she'd be out of a position if Helen regretted her actions. There would never be a place she'd feel as safe and happy than on the grounds of this school.

Not only was the school property men-free overnight, but it taught women to forge their own paths inasmuch as society allowed. And the acceptance of all sorts of sexual preferences 'twas heaven on earth. She wouldn't lie to herself. She hoped to one day meet a life partner. But if she didn't, it would not be the worst thing either. She was far happier here than she had been anywhere else.

Most importantly, any partner had to be someone suitable. And Helen Montague was *not* suitable.

Regina strode back and forth to the field with her charges, her mind in turmoil. To reinforce how lucky she was even without a lover, she reminded herself of the discomfort of her childhood. While she learned to sew and cook, her brother learned riding and repair work. After several years of frustration and too many unpicked stitches, she'd finally borrowed a set of his clothes, bound her budding breasts, and walked several neighborhoods over in their London suburb to hire on as a stable hand.

There, she'd discovered her love of horses. At first, she'd simply wanted to be outdoors rather than stuck in the kitchen with her mother and her friends, listening to them complain about their husbands and children. The physical exertion of caring for the horses appealed to her, and the beasts' gentle nature and intelligence drew her in.

When she returned home with her wages to help the household, her mother stopped questioning where she'd gone, and better yet, stopped asking for her help with the cooking and sewing.

The other stable hands were friendly. They joked about girls they'd tupped, the figures of women who passed on the street, and everything else sexual. Regina found it all far more comfortable than listening to her mother's friends discuss their husbands' prowess.

She suspected she had far more in common with these boys than a sense of humor. However, she daren't act on her feeling so close to home. To do so would bring shame to her family. So she left home, bouncing from stable to stable, finding a few girls willing to experiment and a few others who shared her interests outright.

She worked at a stable next to a London theatre and paused her duties one afternoon a week to observe clusters of women in daring dresses arrive and depart.

She learned from one of the women, who drove a phaeton she paid Regina to care for, that the ladies were courtesans. The women came to meet a matron in the theatre who assisted them with saving their hard-earned funds.

On a spring day, a lady older than most of the others strolled over after many of the courtesans had gone their separate ways. Dressed more moderately, she had a kind smile and soft eyes.

"Hullo." Regina nodded to her and resumed sweeping the wide doorway of the stables. Despite the other woman's welcoming demeanor, Regina's heart pounded. What did this stranger want with her? Her greatest irony was that she was often more comfortable talking to men than to women.

"Hello, dear. My name is Leah Godwin. I am so pleased to meet you…"

"Regina Carlisle at your service, Missus Godwin."

"Oh, call me Leah, please. I often observe you lingering here gazing at the theatre. Are you perhaps considering a career on the stage?"

"Just enjoying the view, ma'am." Regina winked, deliberately being outrageous so this lady would leave her alone and stop asking questions. There was a reason she worked with horses—they required less conversation.

"'Tis Leah, please. Right, then. I am glad we can be of assistance." Leah smiled.

Regina gaped.

Within a month, she'd had tea with Leah several times and had come to love her. One afternoon, Leah described the school and offered her the role of stablemistress.

Now, she'd been here three years and was still a little in shock. Everyone here—literally everyone, or they were asked to leave—accepted her as she was. If she wanted to hack her hair off or wear men's clothes as they were better suited to her role, fine. In the end, she was most comfortable wearing split skirts with broken-in stays. She kept the occasional day dress for when sponsors, mostly men, visited and she interacted with them to handle their mounts.

Their horseflesh, she amended with a chuckle. *Here, "mounts" could be misconstrued.*

Those few years before the school, she'd been lonely, feeling isolated. Sapphic relationships were frowned upon, if not illegal. Thankfully, the laws regarding women's relationships were murkier than those around men's. 'Twas perhaps the one area in which men had less freedom than women. Either way, it was difficult to find like-minded people to form friendships with, never mind intimate relationships.

At school, the staff were all friendly. Still unsure of what she'd have in common with women who were teachers, kitchen staff and housekeepers, she'd taken ages to sit with others at meals. But once she did, she quickly found a circle of women who she liked and admired.

Sure, she missed physical intimacy. There was the occasional liaison with a like-minded housekeeper, but those were few and far between. But she had a form of love here she'd never had before.

Having led the last of the older horses out to pasture, she cleaned and filled their water troughs, keeping watch for Helen's return so she would not be chastised for doing too much. As Helen returned from exercising the third mare, Regina reached the only conclusion she could. Sex with the deliciously soft headmistress was not worth giving up her home and family. She must put this infatuation aside.

* * * *

Helen turned the last of the younger mares toward the stables. The sun's heat stung her nose. Her hat's narrow brim protected her forehead, but she'd look like she had a cold for the next two days. She could not bring herself to care. This had been a much-needed break from the never-ending administrative tasks awaiting her in her office.

On days like this, she was jealous of roles like Regina's. On the other hand, Regina had fallen because her work was the same in much worse weather, when Helen had a lovely fire and a lap blanket over her as she worked.

As she rode into the stable yard, she again admired Regina's strength and sleekness as she hauled buckets of water and food. Her fingertips tingled at the memory of pads of muscles against them, and she squirmed on the saddle. Now that she recognized her attraction to Regina, she could not see past it.

She had no business staring at a member of her staff, even one she'd seen semi-nude. However, it wouldn't hurt to become better acquainted with Regina. She was one of the closest in age to Helen, after all.

The thought of age prompted Helen to recall her thickening waistline and graying hair. Just because Regina preferred the company of women did not mean she'd be attracted to an older, heavier woman. Helen was being conceited to assume otherwise.

No, better they stay friends.

"I thought we'd agreed to leave those heavy buckets for the man from the village?" she teased Regina.

Regina strolled closer to help her dismount with a grin. "I do not recall agreeing to that."

Helen laughed, shaking her head. Slipping one boot out of the saddle, she held the pommel to swing the leg back and over to slide down into Regina's waiting arms. She failed. Sitting awkwardly on the saddle, she made a distressed sound.

Regina walked around the horse's head, holding a lower section of rein, to check what was wrong.

Helen blushed. "'Twas only that I couldn't raise my leg high enough. I may have overdone things a tad."

"Oh. Can I help?"

"No!" Helen's response was quick and slightly horrified. "How embarrassing. And you re-injuring yourself would bely the point of all this exertion on my part."

Regina stifled a giggle and came back around. "Right, then. I shall catch you if you fall."

At that mental image, Helen almost wished to tumble off. However, she'd humiliated herself enough for one day.

Heaving her leg over, she felt Regina's hand at her other ankle, ensuring it was free of the stirrup. Then hands were at her waist, holding her as she slid to safety on the ground.

"There. Perhaps not the most graceful dismount, but I did it. Thank you." She turned, and Regina was so close she could feel the woman's breath across her temple.

Helen clenched her fists, her stomach flip-flopping.

She hoped for a moment like the day before, but Regina stepped back immediately.

"Ta, mistress. She's the last of them for today. I'll see to the saddle and grooming."

Helen opened her mouth, but Regina raised a hand.

"I beg your pardon. I'll have the 'man from the village'—she pitched her tone higher to mimic Helen and finished in her own voice through a grin—"see to the saddle and grooming."

Helen dared to reach for her hand and squeezed it. "One more day, so I don't worry. Please?"

Regina's tongue darted out to wet her lips at the last word, but she remained silent, nodding once.

Helen spent the rest of the day and into the evening forcing herself to concentrate on the many decisions awaiting her on her desk. When her thoughts strayed to the firm arms and engaging laugh of the stablemistress, she ruthlessly squashed them and tackled the next document. As was so often the case in recent weeks, she took her supper on a tray in her office.

Finally, she shoved her chair back, she decided her reward for her hard work would be to see how Regina fared. Only to need three attempts to gain her feet. There would be no walk across the grounds, she'd be lucky to make her own bed.

Chapter Four

On the third morning, Regina was surprised the headmistress had not come to check on her. Or if she was truthful with herself, disappointed.

She'd half expected the older woman the night before. By the morning, she was sneaking glances around as she carried water and food, but there was no sign of Helen. She told herself it was for the best. Her back felt fine, and while she would be careful—at least her version of careful—for another couple days, she was grateful and happy to be back at work.

Grace appeared a quarter hour after classes began. "Is Helen out with a horse?"

Regina barely refrained from jerking in shock. "No. She isn't at her desk?"

The assistant frowned. "I've yet to see her this morning. I know she worked late, but I thought she might be down here helping you."

"Really? Doesn't she usually start early?" Regina blurted out. In trying not to become alarmed, she hadn't considered the fact that there was no good reason for her to know the headmistress's schedule in such detail. She did not know anyone else's work hours.

"Yes, actually. I have to get back so someone is covering the office. I'll send someone to check her quarters."

"No need. I can do it." At Grace's quizzical look,

she tacked on a quick excuse. "You've both spent enough time helping me. I am happy to return the favor."

Shrugging, the younger woman hurried off.

Regina sighed in relief that Grace had not questioned her familiarity with Helen's preferences. Now she had an opportunity to verify Helen's wellbeing like she so kindly had done for Regina. She shook her head and admitted the truth—she simply wanted to see Helen.

She strode purposefully toward the main hall. Grabbing a tray with a pot of tea, two cups, sugar, and milk, she took mincing steps toward Helen's rooms. The items rattled with every step. A housemaid, she'd never be.

Heaving a sigh of relief at not spilling or dropping anything, she used an elbow to knock carefully.

And waited.

She knocked again.

Helen's voice called, "Grace? Let yourself in, please, I can't get up again just now."

Daggers. How was she supposed to open the door whilst holding the infernal tray? Her respect for maids increased proportionately to her efforts to not drop the entire tea service.

Wrestling the tea tray to one forearm and hand with a little help from the doorframe, she bent at the knees to keep the tea from spilling and eased the door open.

A sitting room appeared, all clean and tidy with a settee the color of early peas, a paisley-patterned chair with similar tones, and a dark area rug between them. There was no sign of Helen.

Regina cleared her throat. "Helen? 'Tis Regina, not Grace. I, um, brought tea."

"Regina?" Rustling sounds came from a second doorway behind the still-open door followed by a groan.

Regina jolted in alarm and decided it was in the best interests of Helen's rug and her hands to put down the tea on a side table. Closing the outer door, she ventured closer to what she guessed was the bedroom.

"Thank you ever so much for the tea, Regina. I appreciate it. How is your back feeling?" Helen called out.

"Right as rain, Mistress, ta. Shall I pour?"

"Er, no. I'll be a few minutes, and I don't want to keep you from your day. Shall I visit the stable later perhaps?"

"Grace is concerned." Regina had had enough of the headmistress's prevarications. "Daggers, *I* am concerned. You never begin work this late. It would allay my worries greatly to see for myself that you are hale and healthy."

A sigh emanated from the semi-dark room. "Therein lies the rub. I confess I am not as hale or hearty as I should be."

Alarm propelled Regina to the bedroom. Helen lay prone in a chemise, the bed linens crumpled under her, her legs bare from the knee down.

"What is the matter, Helen?" She rushed over to the bed, not sure what she planned. Checking for a fever? For broken bones?

"Apparently going from zero exercise to riding for several hours is not recommended at my age." Helen's tone was disgruntled, and she was pouting.

Regina raised a hand to hide her grin.

"I can see your smile still, you know." Helen's brows dropped in a mock glare, before she flipped her hand against the bed. "I barely made it to bed last night, and I thought I'd be better today. But it's worse!"

"I understand, and I beg your pardon. I feel as though my carelessness and back pain caused this."

"No, no. This is someone—" she gestured vaguely upward. "—telling me I should be exercising more regularly to avoid this very situation."

"Well, be that as it may, what can I do to help? Can you sit? Tea, perhaps? And moving slowly?"

"I started to dress, but even my fingers hurt. Perhaps you could help me with my stays and whatnot?"

Regina's mind raced. *Do I dare?*

She could play it off as returning the favor. Helen had been matter-of-fact about her offer. But could she hide her feelings if she put her hands on Helen's body?

"Regina?" Helen was watching her, head tilted. She'd been woolgathering too long.

"I was thinking, Mistress." She used Helen's title deliberately to remind herself she needed to proceed carefully, as her livelihood was in the balance. "Wouldn't a rubdown with camphor oil help you as it did me?"

She held her breath waiting for Helen's response. Helen might opt for Grace or someone else, anyway.

"What a splendid idea. George would be so pleased that his back pain would benefit both of us in some way. Would you be so kind?"

Oh my. Regina's hands fluttered. She looked at them in disbelief. What on earth? She'd never been nervous, not even with the first girl she'd gotten naked. From the start, she'd known what she liked, and once she'd received permission to touch, she moved forward with alacrity.

Gathering her wits, she nodded. "Of course. I'll pour you tea, then fetch the camphor oil and let Grace know you're under the weather. Shall I say if she doesn't see you in the office in an hour, she can come check on you?"

"Thank you, that would be lovely."

Tea poured and doctored, she trotted out for the oil and galloped back, obsessing on where Helen was likely hurting and how to preserve a modicum of modesty and professionalism for them both. Panting, she knocked then entered Helen's suite, going straight to the bedroom.

Where Helen lay under the sheet on her belly, her chemise on the floor beside the bed.

Regina's breath whooshed out, and she grabbed for the bedpost.

* * * *

"I hope you don't mind. I thought this would be easier." Helen mumbled against the pillow. After noticing the tightness of her clothes, then Regina's fitness, she'd preferred to struggle out of the chemise without an audience. The sheet would also be easier to move out of the way for Regina.

"No, no. As you said, we are both women, our bodies are the same." Regina's voice was strangled.

"Exactly. Lud, I hope this works as well for me as it did for you and George. I can't imagine sitting immobile in an office chair all day like this. Come. Sit or kneel, whatever makes sense." Her hand patted the bed.

The mattress dipped. Regina stilled, one knee on the bed by Helen's hip.

Helen could not see more detail from her prone

position.

"Where does it hurt, Mistress?"

"You called me Helen the other night. I think perhaps when you're going to be touching me without clothing, you could do that again?" The half of her mouth facing Regina curled in a smirk. "And my thighs, my back, my arms, my-er…that will help."

"Your bottom?" Regina's hands flexed in the corner of Helen's sight.

"Well, yes, but I won't ask you to—"

"'Tis quite all right. Anyone who rides knows how many muscles are in one's posterior. If I am to do this, 'tis worth doing all of it."

Helen caught the flick of Regina's tongue over her lips. The poor woman must be more nervous than she'd realized. "'Tis not necessary. Whatever you are comfortable with." But disappointment shot through her at the thought of Regina not touching her arse, surprising her. It hadn't been a source of stimulation for her with George. Helen mentally stopped herself. Those thoughts were inappropriate.

The sheet was lifted away. Glass clinked as Regina removed the stopper from the vial, then the sound of repeated slicking told her that Regina was rubbing her oil-covered hands together. The smooth-over-rough warmth of her palms settled behind Helen's knees. The friction had warmed the oil and created immediate relief, the callouses at the base of Regina's fingers only hinted at beneath the camphor. The mattress dipped again, and Helen felt the drape of fabric over her calves and a slight rubbing along the outside of her legs. Regina was now straddling her.

Helen sighed with contentment at being under

Regina's care. Regina's fingers tightened on her thigh muscles and dug in. Pain radiated from the spot and she yelped. Regina's fingers continued to travel up and down her thighs and Helen tensed.

"This will help, I promise." Regina's voice was deeper, rougher than normal above her.

"Lud, I forgot how strong you are."

"Shh. Deep breaths."

Helen quieted.

Regina palpitated her thick thighs then slid upward. Her hands spanned the width of Helen's thighs with her fingers wrapped around the outside. They came to rest cupping her ample bottom.

Self-consciousness about her size forgotten, Helen bit a moan back behind her lips.

A near-silent groan rumbled above her as fingers caressed the globes of her bottom.

Helen twitched. These were not the actions of a rubdown, they felt…reverent.

She bit back a moan. Her conscience kept whispering the word *inappropriate*, but the rushing of her blood drowned it out. Whatever this was, she may as well relax and enjoy it. She'd always accepted the tenet that sensual desire could happen between any two or more people, and from the start had ensured that the school was a safe place for both staff and students who wanted to explore that. Having only just discovered her own interest in intimacy was more fluid than she'd realized during her marriage, she would not run from learning more.

She released her moan into the room.

Regina froze. "Did I hurt you? I beg your pardon."

"Oh, no, dear. It all feels wonderful."

"Right, then. I was, er, spreading the oil around." Regina's fingers curled, and her knuckles drove into Helen's squishy bottom cheeks.

"Oh," came out on a sigh. There really were muscles under there somewhere.

"See?" The voice behind her held a smile. Regina's weight leaned into Helen as she prodded her fists into particular knots. Her breath was as fractured as Helen's.

After seconds or perhaps hours, the warm massage moved up her back, and Helen relaxed into it, moaning occasionally in response to muscles being loosened.

Regina's final rubdown was to smooth her hands from Helen's shoulders downward, her thumbs gliding gently on the muscles on either side of her spine. They remained together over her bottom, teasing the crack between her cheeks with the lightest of touches.

Helen's breath caught, and she arched, pushing her bottom up a degree. Her eyes fluttered closed so she needn't meet Regina's undoubtedly questioning look, as her heart raced. What did she want? She wished she knew. Her feelings were new enough that she hadn't had time to consider the logistics of intimacy with a woman—with this woman.

An answering gasp came from Regina and her hands slowed and tightened, dragging the lowest part of Helen's bottom apart an inch.

Helen twitched, her hips still raised an inch.

They both froze for an eternity. Helen wanted to beg, hoping to explore this sudden sensitivity in her arse cheeks. She craved Regina's touch between her thighs delving to find the part of her that didn't need any oil, having created its own lubrication. But these feelings might be borne of loneliness, or physical attraction, while she and Regina might not be compatible outside of bed. Pursuing this any further without more reflection wouldn't be fair to her stablemistress—her *employee*.

Regina recovered and smoothed her hands farther down Helen's thighs before clambering off the bed.

"Remain still, I'll wipe the excess oil off you so it doesn't ruin your clothes."

Helen drifted. Her bottom still felt those thumbs prying her open to Regina's gaze. Her nipples had tightened and chafed against the bed linens.

Regina returned with a damp cloth, which she'd warmed. She wiped everywhere she'd stroked. With her large hands, she'd reached most of the way around Helen's legs. But despite Helen waiting with bated breath, Regina did not brush the cloth up her inner thighs.

Instead, she stepped back and held the cloth out to Helen. "Here—" She cleared her throat. "—I think you can reach the rest. Do you need help sitting?"

Helen placed her hands by her shoulders and pushed up, swinging her legs gingerly toward the edge of the bed. She wasn't pain-free but was far more mobile than she'd been.

Regina gasped yet again.

Helen's gaze shot upward and found the stablemistress's gaze riveted somewhere below her face. Glancing down, she saw why. Her nipples were still tight little buds, her breasts bare as she faced Regina.

Unwilling to contemplate whether her reaction was temperature or Regina-related, she swallowed through a tight throat and reached for her chemise, only to find her hand blocked by Regina's.

"I beg your pardon," Regina stammered, looking up from the chemise. As she'd squatted to get the garment, her gaze was now on a level with Helen's breasts. She raised her head and licked her lips, unable to stop staring.

Right, then. Not temperature-related. This beautiful, brave, younger woman desires me. And I want her.

Their work relationship all but forgotten, Helen searched her memory for her long-dormant flirting skills. In those days, she had never led the progression of a relationship, though. In this case, she'd need to provide some signal to being open, as all Regina knew was that Helen had been married to a man.

Taking a deep breath, she found her inner headmistress lurking deep down and took control of the situation, as she'd trained herself to do these past years running the school.

"They're not bad for over forty, are they?" She forced a light laugh while drawing the chemise over herself.

"They're lovely," burst from Regina before she pressed her lips together with a frown.

"Why thank you, my dear. Now, may I borrow an arm, in case standing does not go as well as sitting, please?"

In the end, she was at her desk within the hour, Regina having helped her dress although refusing to lace her as tightly as she usually wore her stays. Her fingers would only tolerate writing for short stints, but she was able to wade through most of her duties, even as her mind lingered on the strong and caring stablemistress.

* * * *

Regina was exhausted at the end of the day. The stable hand from the village had done most of the heavy lifting the day before, a relief given her preoccupation with her interaction with Helen that morning.

She'd spilled more water than she'd poured into troughs, her focus on her hands and the memory of Helen's skin under them, rather than on what they carried.

Her fatigue was a result of her confusion more than extra trips for water, however. Had she seen desire in Helen's eyes? Had she imagined the arch of Helen's generous bottom under her grip or perhaps wished a reason for it which did not exist? Even the headmistress's flirtatious-sounding comment as she dressed could have been nerves after not having been seen naked for years.

Her weariness might also stem from skipping breakfast to check on Helen and excusing herself for a brief "lunch" during which she ducked into her room to rub her swollen, needy flesh to a small explosion. While not satisfying, it at least took the edge off so she didn't hurt herself with the manual labor of her position.

After the last chores were finished, she had a quarter hour until the supper bell. The stables were deserted, so she performed a quick check-in with her back muscles, because Helen would quiz her whether she was truly ready to ride again.

Lifting herself up with the edge of a stall half-wall, she stepped onto a mounting block that sat in the wide path between stalls for the smaller students. Swinging her right leg up as though to mount, she waited to see if the sharp pains of days ago would return. Her muscles were tight, but there was not even a twinge of pain. After stepping down, she raised one leg to the mounting block, leaned forward in a stretch over it, then did the same with the other. Finally, holding the top of the partition, she twisted and turned, not finding aches.

As she held a twist, a wet nose snuffled on her knuckles. "Hullo, piglet," she said to Henrietta, the mare whose stall wall she'd borrowed. She'd chosen the name because it was more of a sow's name in her mind, and this mare would eat grass until she'd make herself sick. Knowing she was searching for apple slices, Regina produced one and held her palm out for the horse to gobble happily.

She laughed and patted the mare before bending at the waist to touch her toes, doing one last stretch and check.

Hearing an intake of breath behind her, she shot to standing and whirled. Helen stood staring at where her bottom had been. As the headmistress's gaze climbed to meet hers, Regina had the passing thought that if the whirl hadn't hurt, she was ready for anything.

Helen's deep brown gaze, with her pupils dilated, caused a different muscle to twinge. Her heart…with hope.

Chapter Five

Despite starting late, Helen ended her workday earlier than normal. She'd only get further behind if she did not take the time to sort through her confusion and decide her next actions. Whether she was comfortable with it or not, she was attracted to her stablemistress. And unless she misinterpreted the signs of interest, Regina felt a similar pull.

Helen knew herself. Some men and women treated sexual intimacy as scratching an itch, but she could not. She'd been in love with George before their relationship became physical. She had the utmost respect for Regina; the woman kept the stables running seamlessly and had never once asked for repairs or outside help or even a horse doctor. Helen had been impressed before she'd discovered how heavy the water buckets were. But while her emotions were already engaged, she didn't know the stablemistress well, and the last thing she wanted was tension between her and a staff member when their dalliance ended.

Had Regina simply enjoyed touching a nude female form—in other words, her availability? After all, the stablemistress was younger and far more fit than she was.

Even if she held an allure for Regina, they worked together. The school had firm rules about more than friendship between managers and staff, and teachers and students—basically, any situation in which one had direct power over the other's experience at the institution. She was a prime example of that decree, as she only reported to the board of overseers. She could not take advantage of her role. Helen recognized that she was the person in power. Regina would be loath to act on any interest with a superior.

On the other hand, she wondered when the stablemistress had last had sex. The concern that their attraction was opportunistic would not dissipate.

She shook her head to stop her thoughts from going around in circles.

When in doubt, communication was the key to understanding. She'd talk to Regina. She wanted to check whether they needed help from the village again the next day anyway.

She arrived at the stable in time to see a laugh light up Regina's face, her generous lips pulling wide, her simple ponytail falling down her back as she tilted her head to a mare's. She was always pretty but she was downright gorgeous when she laughed.

The stablemistress bent, folding in half with the shape of her rear outlined. Recalling the texture of smooth skin over firm muscles from the other night, Helen sucked in a breath.

Regina snapped up and around to stare at her.

"Good evening." Helen stepped toward her with a smile. "Dare I hope these contortions mean you're feeling better?"

The taller woman flushed and nodded. "How did you fare today, Mistress?"

Helen tsked. "'Tis Helen, remember? I was thankful I did not need to ride today, but I was able to move about well enough, particularly if I did not sit still too long."

"I am glad."

"Have you eaten?"

"No, but I aim to as soon as the bell sounds."

"I'd like to talk with you, if I may. Privately. Would you be amenable to having a private meal in a meeting room?"

"Certainly. Let me freshen up and I can join you outside your office in a quarter hour?"

Helen wished Regina had agreed to go immediately, so she would not spend long minutes dithering with nerves. She hadn't experienced these feelings since George had wooed her twenty-five years ago, and she hated that she felt like a silly eighteen-year-old. Apparently, coquetry never aged.

Twenty minutes later, she stood to greet Regina and gestured her to a seat across from Helen's. The table was only slightly larger than Regina's and was covered in a tablecloth with matching serviettes. The soup course had been served and their wineglasses filled, but Helen had placed the carafe on a cabinet against the wall. She wanted her wits about her for this conversation, as it required finesse.

"Mistr—Helen. I confess to some concern about this private meeting. Did I overstep this morning?"

Helen jerked in surprise and reached across to pat Regina's hand, white-knuckled around her wine glass. "Oh goodness, no. I am so sorry, I did not mean to be cryptic." She gulped. It was now or never. "I should like to become better acquainted."

Regina looked skeptical.

"I understand your suspicion. We've worked together for three years. Why now?" At the other woman's nod, she continued, "'Tis too easy, here in the main building, to focus on the classes and, of course, the recruiting of both teachers and students. Then there are the investors to report to and the sponsors to deal with. These past few days have given me much more appreciation for the work that needs to be done elsewhere as well."

Regina's expression smoothed out. She was willing to listen, even if she remained frozen in her seat.

Phew.

A kitchen staff member brought in baked herbed fish with root vegetables and removed their soup bowls.

After she'd left, Helen continued. "More than that, however, was the realization that we have much in common. I know I could benefit from your friendship if you're willing."

The stablemistress arched a dubious brow.

"Look around you," Helen rushed on, determined to win her over. "Several of the instructors are married and live in the village. The ones who are single are generally younger. We are—ahem—more mature. We are both dedicated to our roles here and love the school. More than that, circumstances have given us an opportunity to get to know each other better." She nearly swallowed her tongue on the word "better." At least she hadn't said "naked."

This is scary. How do men—or women—do this?

She was only attempting it because she truly desired to become closer to Regina and explore options of friendship or, ideally, more. She said some of that wish out loud, finishing with, "I'd like to continue."

"True," Regina drew the word out, tilting her head. "What did you have in mind?"

Helen coughed and swept her hand around the

room. "Supper, to start."

Regina's shoulders lowered the last inch, and she leaned back in her chair. "What would you like to know?"

Helen stuttered to a halt. She hadn't gotten that far in her planning. Of course, she wished to learn if Regina was as interested in kissing her as Helen was in being kissed, but that wasn't a starting point.

Regina was waiting for an answer.

"I am not sure where to begin," she admitted. "I supposed I can't ask you what you dislike most about your workplace, in case you expect me to fix it." A nervous titter of laughter escaped, taking her by surprise.

Regina laughed, her eyes alight, charming Helen again as it had in the stable. Still grinning, she answered, "Actually, you can. There is nothing I dislike about my workplace aside from the weather, and that you cannot control."

"I'll ask again when we've had more time together. I wonder whether you're simply being polite now."

"Mistress—Helen—here is the first thing to know about me. I am terrible at observing the proprieties. You'll get truth from me always. I'll couch it as politely as possible, of course, but I do not hem and haw."

"That is good to know, particularly as I am the same. 'Tis always a trial to deal with difficult sponsors and their unreasonable requests."

"Better you than me." Regina nodded.

A kitchen worker rolled a cart in with pudding and tea and cleared their dishes.

Helen poured them each a cup.

"Ta," Regina thanked her. "You know, given your long hours at a desk and how sore you were from a few short rides—"

Helen gasped in mock outrage.

Regina snickered at her expression before continuing. "—perhaps on the nicer days we can ride together whilst we become better acquainted?"

"That sounds marvelous," Helen said with a vigorous nod.

And perhaps I'll earn another chance at your hands on me.

* * * *

The next several days were rainy, and one of them Helen ended up working late, but she managed to invite Regina for a few private evening meals. Regina wandered around the stables talking to her babies in the afternoons between chores, in case the headmistress managed time to walk down and issue the invitation personally. Even when the offer came via a note carried by a student, it never failed to lift her spirits. She felt giddy. Her crush hovered so close to a real tryst she could taste it, yet she daren't act on it.

During the first evening meal, both women peeled back another layer of themselves.

Helen had grown up only a short ride from the school grounds. When her sister Teresa had gone to London to work at a charity school, she'd visited and learned she was not suited for the rules and noise of city living. The open space of meadows and smell of the forests near her home were her preference. She returned home and married George, a man from the next village, joining him on his parents' farm. They were happy for almost two decades before he died of infection from a plowing injury. As he had no siblings, he ensured that Helen inherited the land.

Regina shared her childhood in London as well as her past employment there, and agreed with Helen's opinion of London. Her affection for horses meant she'd always prefer to live where they'd be more comfortable, in turn adding to her happiness.

The next supper brought a deeper layer of questions. "What do you miss most from your marriage?" Regina asked Helen. Never having more than a few stolen hours or nights with any one person made her curious.

"It depends on the day, to be honest. Occasionally there will be a jar I can't open, or a repair needed. Mostly, I miss the companionship of sharing space with someone I love, who knows me inside and out, and whom I know equally well. There is nothing like that in the world."

"I can't imagine," Regina's wistfulness echoed in her voice.

Helen slid her a sly look. "Well, and sex."

Regina choked, caught between laughter and surprise. "That, I can imagine. I've never had a real relationship, though. The need for secrecy in London and the challenge of finding like-minded women made it hard. Between my preferred profession and my overall lack of femininity, there wasn't much opportunity."

Helen smacked the table and gritted out, "I never want to hear you say something like that again. You've worked here for three years so you know better. First, everyone is beautiful. 'Tis the first tenet we teach here. Second, do not buy into society's definition of femininity. Make your own, and live by it."

Shocked, Regina watched her carefully.

"It seems like you have done that for the most part," Helen continued in a softer tone. "You manage a physically and mentally demanding post better than anyone I could imagine. And—" she gulped, "—I find you lovely."

Ignoring the happy thump in her chest, Regina didn't know how to take Helen's words. Finally, she curled up one side of her mouth and said, "Yes, well, that is only half the equation."

"Perhaps not. The school teaches all of us to be open-minded." Helen's return smile flickered with uncertainty.

Regina was speechless, unsure how to respond, and the talk turned to their tasks for the next day.

The following night, Regina asked Helen how she continued work after dark, and the headmistress showed Regina her office. Oil lamps surrounded a small, cleared space on her desk. The remainder of the desk and a sideboard were covered in heaps of paper.

"Helen, this is a fire hazard," she'd exclaimed, shocked and a little frightened.

"Nonsense. I am careful. I do not leave the room with even so much as a candle lit. I am trying to hire another assistant, but that requires trips to London to interview, which puts me further behind and…" She shrugged.

"My word. I have no idea how you keep things straight."

"There is a method to my madness, I promise, and Grace helps. I am glad the days are getting longer, so I can more easily take daylight hours to ride with you. If 'tis clear, I hope to come in the morning once breakfast is over and classes are in session if the offer still stands?"

"Gladly."

"Right, then. I shall see you after breakfast."

* * * *

Regina had two of the feistier horses ready the next morning. Refusing to admit she hoped Helen would be sore again, she took her on a particularly long path around the grounds. Kicking her mount into a canter, she glanced over her shoulder.

The headmistress gamely followed and came up alongside Regina as she slowed to a trot. She admired Helen's form as her thighs gripped the horse and her bosom bounced despite tightly laced stays. The smile on Helen's lips lit up her face and took off the years of worry and work. Regina's own sensitive flesh swelled against the impact of the saddle as she posted. Suddenly aware of her own breasts bouncing, she sucked in a breath, tightening her grip on the reins while being careful not to tug on them.

Helen beamed that smile at her, happily oblivious to Regina's desire to strip her naked and caress every inch of her right there on the bridle path.

The rest of the day was a blur, Regina performing her duties by rote, until a student came with a note from the headmistress inviting her to a private meal again.

Surprised Helen could afford the time given their morning ride, she nonetheless washed and changed to a clean gown and strode the path to the meeting room they used for their meals.

Helen was already seated and did not rise to meet her as she had in the past.

Hmm. She recalled the challenging path she'd

chosen. A devilish hope lit a spark within her.

"I was starving after all the exercise today, so supper is already on its way," Helen said while pouring wine in their glasses.

Regina assessed her movements for stiffness from the ride but saw none. Finally deciding she was overthinking it, and the headmistress was no longer standing on formalities at this point in their friendship, she relaxed to enjoy the meal.

As they dined on lamb roast and the first spring vegetables from the school's greenhouse, Helen regaled her with stories of the craziest requests from sponsors. No names were mentioned and Regina could only guess at some of the students involved, but the stories were entertaining nonetheless. The one she found most perplexing was not even the most outrageous. A husband asked if he could bring two friends to "practice" with his wife during the usual visit toward the end of each program. Of course, this was allowed but only with a school monitor and an open door. The gentlemen and lady did not care. Regina still shook her head at that one, never having been with one man, much less three at once.

After supper, Helen usually walked with Regina as far as the staff quarters in the main building, which was on the way to the side door leading toward the stables.

Regina took her time at the end of the meal before rising. She lay her serviette by her plate with deliberation and raised her glass to her lips to search out every last drop of wine, watching Helen from the corner of her eye.

Helen's actions were slow, also. Unlike her normal graceful exit, she placed both hands on the table and pushed herself up, biting her lip as she did.

Regina rose and faced the older woman. "You

overdid it. You are sore again."

Helen nodded and bit her lower lip.

Regina's blood surged at the sight.

"Perhaps—" Helen gulped "—if you have time…"

Helen's eyes all but begged for Regina's touch. If only 'twas the touch Regina had in mind. "I would be happy to help you again. Would you like my arm?" She proffered a bent elbow as a man might, so Helen could lean on her a bit for the walk to her apartment. Regina's heart raced.

Helen accepted. Her smooth palm, so unlike Regina's own calloused ones, warmed Regina's forearm through the fabric of her dress. Her pulse thrummed in her veins, her breasts and nether lips swelling with desire.

In Helen's bedroom, she helped the headmistress unlace her gown and stays, her fingers fumbling from nerves. Her chest heaved as she gulped breaths. Every muscle strained to take a half-step forward to bring her flush against Helen's back, to smell her hair, to reach around and cup her breasts. With a last inhale, she forced herself to take a step back, pivoting toward the door.

"I'll fetch the camphor oil, shall I?"

"Er, I took the liberty of stocking some here in case I should need it." Helen gestured to her dresser as she moved about the room lighting tapers.

Could Helen have been planning this since the last time? Regina daren't hope. She was no doubt reading too much into things again. What if she wasn't, though? Someone had to be brave.

She glanced up from the crucible as Helen's chemise floated to the floor in her side vision. Sucking in a silent breath, she swallowed at the sight of the rounded arse and thighs offered as Helen bent to fold the bed linens back. Salivating at the quick profile glimpse of heavy breasts as the headmistress climbed onto the bed, Regina stepped forward.

This woman, this leader of women, had been teasing her with her brain and body for a sennight, and Regina was already wet. She needed only the smallest of signs to act on her arousal. A look like the week before would be more than enough.

No. Your income and home rely on Helen's good graces. Be careful.

But she was done being careful. She sat in a small chair in the corner and unlaced her boots. Feeling Helen's gaze on her legs, she did not allow herself to look up in case her hopes had gotten the best of her.

She stood, stepped to the bed and raised her skirts.

Helen's gasp confirmed that this connection wasn't only in Regina's imagination.

Putting one knee near Helen's hip, Regina threw her other leg over to straddle Helen's thighs again, just below her delicious arse.

Helen had not bothered with the sheet this time, another excellent sign.

Regina held her skirts high enough to avoid kneeling on them, and now fluffed them back to pool around her as she lowered herself, so they would not catch under her bottom. Thus her bare nether parts hovered between Helen's thighs.

She hoped her arousal wouldn't spill onto Helen's leg. That would be nigh impossible to explain—or return to simple friendship after.

Candlelight flickered over Helen's alabaster shoulders, and Regina's silhouette cast a diagonal shadow over her bottom and lower back.

Smooth skin over softness was Regina's weakness. She wanted to wilt with longing over Helen's prone form.

Helen moaned.

With a small shift, Regina moved her shoulder out of the path of one of the tapers. Honey glistened on Helen's pouty swollen folds between her legs.

Regina shuddered, afraid to let her hope free. Her previous thought was wrong. A simple look was not enough to risk her future. She needed a clear declaration of interest.

Helen had levered up on her elbows and twisted around to look at her.

"Regina." Her voice was lower, with gravel in it.

"Helen. What do you want?"

"I want…" Helen took a deep breath. "I want you."

Regina's core flooded at the words, but she had to be sure. This school taught an enlightened approach to intimacy, but as far as she knew, Helen had only ever been interested in men.

"Do you mean a massage?"

"If that is what you are comfortable with. I am interested in more caresses than a massage involves, but only if it suits you." Helen was blushing but held her gaze.

"What about"—her hand flipped over and back again on Helen's arse—"your husband?"

"He's dead these past few years, dear." Helen grinned at her.

"You know what I mean."

"I think you mean, am I going to close my eyes and pretend you're hairier and sport a cock? Or that I'm doing this because I am lonely and wanting a tup and you're convenient?" Helen pushed against Regina and rolled over to face her. Her full, bountiful breasts mounded on her ribcage. "No. I want you. My new friend, who has impressed me with her caring nature, her humorous conversations with her charges, her strength, and her beauty. My eyes shall stay open the whole time. Just because I have not tried this before does not mean I don't want to. I simply may need a bit of guidance."

Regina nearly swooned for the first time in her life. Her hands hovered, wanting to weigh those gorgeous breasts in her palms while simultaneously wishing to dive between those glinting folds. Licking her lips, she asked, "Can I make you feel good? Can I…touch you?"

Chapter Six

"Yes, please. I would very much like to touch you, also." Helen answered breathlessly.

With every step toward her rooms, her body had heated another degree, her stiffness from the ride forgotten. But Regina's offer was too tempting to pass up. If a massage was all that came of this, she'd be happy with that.

As she undressed, sparks flew from fingers to toes, from breasts to the secret place between her legs. The tendrils of desire were like long-lost friends she'd missed these past years, yet entirely new. A new lover, in particular this person she already cared for, gave an edge of uncertainty to the intimacy Helen welcomed.

Regina's question made her breathe a sigh of relief, even as her arousal spiked higher with the knowledge it would soon be sated.

Regina shook her head. "'Tis not necessary. Tonight is about you."

"Hmm. We shall see." Helen had learned plenty of ways to lead in her role, and sometimes, the best approach was biding one's time. Meanwhile, she was eager to enjoy Regina's attentions.

Regina quickly shed her clothes and resumed her position straddling Helen. She placed her hands on Helen's hips and slid them slowly up to cup her breasts. Her teeth caught her lower lip, and her focus on where her fingertips traced was absolute.

Helen sucked in a breath, ready to squirm and beg. More, she wanted a closer connection to reflect the emotions that welled within her. She'd missed hugs and kisses in widowhood as much as she'd missed sex. She leaned up and slid a hand under Regina's dark hair to tug her closer. Their lips met, and Helen shivered with passion, fleetingly noting the happy absence of stubble. Then she could only process sensation and the heady combination of the familiar act of kissing with new elements. Soft lips, hot tongue, and perhaps best of all, breasts against her own.

She fell back, and Regina followed her down, her hair curtaining around them as their kiss continued. Helen's hands roamed her back, cataloging the smooth satin of her skin over firm pads of muscle.

When Regina's fingers skimmed down her much softer stomach again, she flinched.

Regina raised her head. "Helen? What is it? Did I hurt you?"

"No. You are young and firm and fit. I am a lump of dough that has sat too long. I am a bit self-conscious."

Regina straightened to straddle her hips and stare at her. "You are lovely. I have wanted you almost since our first meeting. I like my women soft. Heck, most men do, so I consider myself lucky not to have to worry about my muscles."

They both chuckled.

"Really?" Helen checked, gripping Regina's muscled thighs, kneading their firmness as she devoured the sight of soft breasts and skin over the firmness of Regina's toned body.

"Really. Now, shush. My mouth has better things to

do for the moment. Did you think I only wanted to touch with my hands?" She wiggled her eyebrows.

Helen sucked in a breath, her heart missing a beat.

Regina's gaze shot to her breasts at the movement.

Exhaling on a sigh of pleasure, Helen relaxed and took another deep inhale, accepting the other woman's attraction.

Regina proceeded to worship—there was no other word for it—Helen's soft body with her lips following her fingers, until Helen was writhing on the bed and begging.

"Please. I cannot handle any more."

Planting an elbow by her thigh, Regina lay between her legs. Her thumb swirled at Helen's opening before moving up to the tight bundle of nerves as two fingers slid slowly inside of her.

Lightning shot from those fingers up Helen's spine. She froze, part in pleasure and part because it was a tight fit. Her core teetered between arousal and pain.

Regina stilled her movements. Lifting her thumb, she blew on Helen's nub.

"Ah," Helen squeaked.

Regina's cheek shifted against her inner thigh in a smile.

Feeling brave, Helen bucked her hips up an inch, driving against the invading fingers.

Regina blew again, then flattened her tongue against that sensitive protrusion.

Helen nearly exploded without any further friction. Panting, she ran a hand over Regina's hair.

Tongue flicks ensued, and her hips thrust in counterpoint. Heat coiled in her core, and she moaned.

Of course, she'd given herself pleasure, but after the

first months of missing her husband, desire had waned. She'd assumed it was age, and focused her energies on her work. Self-induced orgasms were pony rides to the full-blown gallop of this, however.

Tension built and blood flowed, centered on her lover's interest in her most sensitive flesh. "Ohmyword, ohmyword, ohmyword," she chanted.

Regina rose to kneel, her lips wet, and Helen moaned anew at seeing the evidence of her own arousal, barely following Regina's next words. "I want to see you go over."

Regina's thumb swiped once, twice. She twisted her hand and pressed her thumb into Helen's quivering nub while her fingers pistoned in and out.

After only one thrust, Helen set her jaw and keened. An explosion of pleasure racked her from head to toe, snapping her spine taut. Her hands clenched and unclenched against the bedcovers, and her eyelids curtained her view of Regina's satisfied yet hungry gaze.

The finger movements against her gentled, and she loosened her muscles one by one as her brain drifted toward awareness.

Eyes fluttering open, she smiled at her lover.

Regina sat back and sucked her fingers into her mouth.

A little spasm of rapture caught Helen off guard. Those digits had been inside her a moment ago. She took advantage of the woman's distraction and sat up, pushing her sideways to lie on the bed.

"My turn."

* * * *

Regina was on fire watching Helen derive sensual satisfaction at her hands and lips.

She'd sat back to savor her partner's essence, sucking on her fingers, the salty musky flavor further igniting her passion.

Then the room tilted, and she found herself on her back, Helen looming over her with a satisfied smirk, her demand ringing in Regina's ears.

"You don't have to." Regina couldn't believe the words that escaped her. She was so on edge that she didn't need an expert touch to explode. Her skin was itchy, craving friction from Helen's soft sweetness. Her core pulsed, wanting to grind against Helen's leg. There was no reason to not let Helen explore and discover new pleasures.

"What was it you said earlier? Hush. My mouth has better things to do than argue with you." Helen grinned.

"Right, then. Hushing underway. Please go about your business." Regina lay back and gave a languid wave, chuckling.

Helen knelt astride her much as Regina had for her. Running her hands from forearms up to shoulders, down to belly, and finally along the long legs stretched out behind her. She seemed to be learning Regina's body.

If she let herself think about it too much, Regina might cry. She'd never felt so admired, so cared for. Swallowing those thoughts back, she focused on the physical. Crying was never conducive to encouraging lovers to return for more.

Twisting into Helen's touches, she exulted in the headmistress's silky hands caressing everywhere. While she loved attention on her breasts, she was of the firm belief that any part of a person could become carnal if touched the right way, with the appropriate intention.

Helen stilled her roaming hands, and planted them on the bed by Regina's shoulders, leaning down to kiss her again. Cushioned lips met hers, tongue seeking.

Helen pulled back. "You taste like me."

"Yesss." Satisfaction rang in her answer.

"It's strange."

"Good strange or bad strange?"

"Just strange. I haven't tasted myself in a long while." Helen ducked her head.

"Do you want me to sip some wine for a moment? The flavor isn't for everyone."

"Well, now, I don't know yet, do I? I have nothing to compare it to—yet." Helen gave her one last short kiss before sliding down her body.

Regina dithered, nervous. Helen had only been with her husband, but she had no idea how adventurous they'd been.

From former lovers who'd been with both genders, she understood this was considered by most to be the biggest difference of physical intimacy with men versus women. The folds, the taste, the challenge of finding the tiny little bundle of nerves. Men were easy. She did not want Helen to be put off.

If she is, do you want her as a partner?

She wasn't sure, but the learning curve did not all have to be mastered in one night.

In the end, she'd thought too hard for too long.

Helen's mouth hit her hot needy flesh as the rest of her soft form settled along Regina's legs.

"Daggers. Helen." She dug her fingers into her thick blond-gray hair.

"Show me what you like."

Ever the demanding headmistress.

Regina chuckled as she parted her lips with one hand, and thrummed her hard kernel with a finger from her other hand.

"On either side to start. Then faster and a bit harder right on the clitoris."

Helen appeared riveted. With a shiver, she looked up and met Regina's gaze along the length of her front.

Regina had never seen anything sexier. She could not recall a single other lover, no one younger, prettier, or more skilled. There was only Helen and *now*.

"Please, touch me?" She, who had never begged in her life, was begging. She'd always been the one to control the experience, being stronger and taller, and therefore assumed to be in charge. This new vulnerability was strange and scary, but delicious.

Especially when Helen's tongue and fingers met at her entrance and mimicked her motions of a second ago.

Her hands fell away, and she gave herself over to sensation.

Within seconds, ecstasy soared, and she clenched, her stomach muscles mounding, her toes curling, as she held Helen gently against her, whispering, "Mistress."

* * * *

Helen did not sleep that night.

Regina had cradled her in her arms, thanking her between kisses and long soothing caresses down her back. Helen had returned them happily. Sleepy, she was slow to register Regina's actions when she climbed off the bed, dressed, gave Helen a last kiss, and let herself out to return to her own room.

Helen lay, bereft, alone in rapidly-cooling sheets that still smelled of Regina. She'd only ever been intimate with George, and they'd shared a bed. It had taken her months to sleep through the night after his death. In some ways, she considered sleeping together more vulnerable but also more satisfying than sex itself.

Perhaps not to Regina.

For the rest of the night, she itemized all the risks in their relationship. While she'd never participated in managing the stables, she'd hired Regina. The stablemistress, like everyone else there, essentially worked for her.

She ran through the students' sponsors, past and present. Their tuition payments were what kept the place running. More importantly, their word of mouth brought in new students. Of course, she had alumnae and other associates quietly recruiting, but that alone would not sustain the costs to run the programs. But if the headmistress herself was in a relationship that, at least on paper, was illegal, there was a bigger risk of alienating would-be sponsors. It wasn't like she was a Ton member with a lady's companion who could hide a deeper relationship under the guise of propriety.

Beyond that, it was against the rules of the school. She recalled the discussion.

"What of romantic entanglements between faculty?" a countess had asked in one of the founders' conversations.

"We are designing this to teach young women to own their own destinies. Shouldn't we lead by example and allow instructors to do the same?" Helen had responded with her own question.

Her sister, now the headmistress at the London

charity school, shook her head. "Managing one's own life, whether the financial or intimate aspects, could be put in jeopardy if someone with power over one's performance at the school took advantage."

"The property is somewhat isolated, with only a village outside its gates and two others more than an hour's ride away." Helen voiced her concern with a frown. After all, she'd be responsible for recruiting and retention of all employees. "Staff will feel isolated there if they must worry every friendship is being scrutinized."

Teresa nodded. "I understand. We need a compromise. Perhaps staff may—" she searched for the word "—comingle—"

The countess snorted.

"—except managers?"

Helen pondered this. "Perhaps only managers and their direct employees are prohibited from—"

"Comingling?" the countess interjected and nearly fell out of her chair laughing.

"Keeping company with each other romantically." She flapped a hand at the countess with a smile. "Or whatever wording you think best."

Helen's lips twisted as she lay in the darkness. That rule definitely applied to Regina and her.

What have I done? Will Regina care if I decline further intimacies?

She almost wished she'd been the scratching of an itch for Regina. It would make things simpler, easier.

Helen sighed into the darkness. That wouldn't make it easier for her. She'd known before their private meal and conversation that she'd only be tempted by someone she cared for, and she wanted more than friendship with the fascinating stablemistress. However, pursuing a deeper relationship would risk the school's future, not just her own. Instead, they were reduced to sneaking around in the darkness. Why had she not thought this through before acting on her attraction? It was one thing to bend the rules, but she could not risk everything she'd worked so hard to build. Nor was it fair to ask Regina to remain a secret.

By dawn, she had exhausted all imaginings of how to make such a partnership work with her role at the school. Determined to be as fair as possible to the other woman, she stumbled through the day in a haze of fatigue and despair. She ate with the students and staff in the main dining room after sending a note to Regina that she would come out to the stables later.

Picking her way down the path, Helen rehearsed what she'd say. Swallowing hard against tears, she took a fortifying breath and swung into the open corridor running between stalls.

Regina paced at the other end, hair gleaming, in her fanciest dress, the navy one she'd worn to their second private supper, after Helen had reassured her about the purpose of those meals.

She looked up and smiled when Helen rounded the doorway.

Helen's heart twisted.

Focused on the need to do what was right, Helen captured her stare but was unable to return her smile.

Regina's expression dropped to a more neutral façade, but she cast a hungry gaze up and down Helen's form.

A spurt of warmth arrowed down from Helen's heart to her core. Two orgasms the night before were apparently not enough to sate her lust for Regina.

However, she could not let this continue. She did not want to hurt Regina more than she needed to.

Sighing, she approached and went on tiptoe to kiss Regina's cheek.

Regina shifted and met Helen's lips with her own.

Helen forgot her worries about being seen, falling into the kiss with body, mind, and soul. She poured her attraction, her sorrow, her respect, and her guilt into Regina's mouth.

After a long moment, Regina broke the kiss, leaning her forehead against Helen's. "Hullo."

"Hello. I missed you."

My word, where did that come from?

Regina grinned at her. "I bet you missed me. Which part?"

Helen giggled once, but sobered to ask, "Can we talk in your apartment?"

"Is that what we're going to call it?"

Chapter Seven

"I wish. Sadly, 'tis not a euphemism. I do need to speak with you."

"Ah." Regina's tone was resigned. She'd known it was too good to last. Her only hope was that she could keep her position. After all, before the past few days, Helen had hardly ever come to the stables.

She held the door for the headmistress, then offered tea or wine, which she'd restocked for that night's visit.

Declining, Helen dithered for a moment before opting for the small table and chairs rather than her only other option, the bed. Once seated, she stared at the table as though gathering her thoughts.

Regina sat across from her.

Helen's eyes gleamed with unshed tears.

Regina had understood all along that theirs could never be more than a short, secret dalliance. She reached across to clasp the headmistress's hand resting on the table.

Helen startled.

"Hey," Regina's voice was gentle. "'Twill be all right. I promise. Whatever it is."

Helen gave a wan smile. "I suppose. You seem to have thought it through more than I did."

"Perhaps. I expect 'tis more that I've been aware of the risks and rewards much longer than you've needed to be."

"How have I run this school without that knowledge?" Helen flung out a hand. "Actually, never mind. That is a conversation for another day, although I value your thoughts on the subject. Right now, 'tis more important to talk about us."

For all her sympathy, Regina needed to know. "Is there an 'us?'"

Helen's lips twisted. "I do not know."

Regina nodded. "I understand."

"'Tis not right that you are sympathetic." Helen frowned. "This is my dilemma, and something I should have considered before I went so far. I don't want to hurt you. I don't want to lose you. Yet I don't see a way to keep you."

Regina's head jerked in stunned surprise, a grin threatening. Helen had some desire to *keep* her? She wanted to smile, dance, maybe even giggle. Reality swiftly beat back that urge, however. Besides being against the rules, an open workplace relationship was a terrible idea, promoting all sorts of talk of favoritism.

"Regina, I cannot lose you when I've just found you." More tears welled in Helen's eyes, and her voice rasped as she continued to clutch Regina's hand. "What shall we do? Meals and friendship? Tiptoeing around is not fair to you, not when you could find someone else. I had expected to be alone after George died. I still do. The school has always been enough for me. It will simply have to be again."

"Hey, hey. Please don't cry. Truly, 'twill be all right." Regina cupped her love's face and swiped her thumb across a cheek to erase the tear streaks. "If you prefer to return to suppers and friendship, that is what we shall do. However, I cannot promise I won't undress you with my eyes every chance I get."

Helen sniffed, one side of her mouth tipping up in a half-hearted smile.

Regina stood and poured them both wine.

Helen accepted hers with a shaky hand and gulped her first taste.

Sitting again, Regina dared to push her preference. "On the other hand, I never expected a public declaration and avowal of forever. And I am accustomed to sneaking around. So, if you have any interest in continuing this, I would be amenable—nay, delighted—to accommodate you."

"How can I even contemplate breaking the rules when I am the ultimate enforcer of them?" Helen wrung her hands. "'Tis not right—"

Regina held up a hand. "Consider the fact that we have never had to have a work-related conversation in the past. The stables have always been self-sufficient."

Helen's shoulders slumped and she took another large sip of wine. "True, but I still cannot fathom circumventing a code of conduct I helped create."

"I have more to lose than you do. If you want to try it for a time, then we shall simply be very careful. But—" she swallowed against her biggest fear. "—whenever it ends, should you feel the need to separate more completely, I would ask for a letter of reference and perhaps some assistance finding a new position."

"What! I would *never* force someone to leave their post for me." Helen straightened in her chair, her voice indignant. "I would only ever terminate someone's employment for due cause, and I cannot imagine that happening with you."

"Well, there is due cause if I knowingly break the

rules with you."

"Right. I am sorry. I understand your concern. Frankly, 'tis one of the reasons for the rule. You have my word I will not ask you to leave the school for personal reasons."

"Thank you. Now, then. If I do need anything, I can discuss it with Grace. She'll be impartial, and if she can't solve it, she'll present it to you as an intermediary."

Helen nodded.

"And"—Regina could not stop her mouth from ticking up on one side—"I think you need a few more samples before you decide what you want."

Helen hummed, her own smile growing. "I see what you mean. I do think I need to more fully explore my options."

Regina's grin nearly split her face. She stood and grabbed Helen's hand to tug her up next to her. "Right, then. Let me show you what is next."

* * * *

Helen hummed as she pulled the last document of the day toward her on the desk.

The piles of paperwork were almost as high and plentiful as always. However, inspired by finding time in the evenings to spend with Regina, she was decisive and efficient on duties that required her judgment. She also had delegated even more tasks to Grace this past fortnight.

Her friendship with Regina was not secret. The staff knew they supped together in a private room. However, Helen had begun to dine with teachers and other employees as well, one at a time, occasionally, to demonstrate fairness. She'd found it surprisingly refreshing to hear about individuals' challenges and goals in a more relaxed ambiance than a formal meeting. Layering personal conversations with professional roles also strengthened her view of the staff as a unit, and balanced the isolation of her endless reams of paperwork.

When Cecilia commented that it was nice to see her form a friendship with Regina given their similar ages, she breathed a sigh of relief. They were doing well at hiding in plain sight.

Guilt continued to plague Helen, but she justified their relationship as portraying a friendship in an isolated existence where close bonds were difficult to develop. Many of their activities were in full view of others. They rode when Helen's schedule allowed it or when she ignored her responsibilities for an hour or two. And there was always a staff member serving their food.

Any time Helen's conscience asked about the future, she shoved the thought away, refusing to dwell on it. She could not bear the idea of nights without Regina. Infatuation and friendship had blossomed into more, as she'd known they would. She was quickly falling for the beautiful stablemistress and would have to spend some time considering how to juggle that with her duties, but for now she simply wanted to bask in the newness of it all.

At meals, they dismissed the staff once pudding was served and carried their own plates back to the kitchen. Their conversation during the first courses were about their workdays, students of particular interest, or innocuous escapades from their past. The last course, or post-dinner sherry if they declined a sweet, was for more intimate conversation.

Regina had shared a bit about her past relationships and the challenges of being a woman not interested in fripperies or traditionally female pursuits, but intensely interested in women themselves.

Helen, in turn, described the pros and cons of a twenty-year relationship and her grief at their apparent inability to have children.

One evening, Helen confided her dreams for the school. "I want to find a way to encourage girls from farther afield to come here. Whilst it must remain secret, I hope that, to the alumnae and sponsors, this will become the alternative to Oxford or Cambridge for their daughters, perhaps from even as far as the Continent."

Regina raised her brows. "From what little I understand of it, the curriculum seems quite different."

"Ah, but think of our alumnae. They are already learning the law, medicine, and all manner of business. As they become more learned, perhaps some will return to teach, and the advanced course will have a broader scope. There might be intermediate classes, as well as more specialized programs like our mercantile training." She stared into space considering it for a moment before shaking her head to return to the present.

Regina was watching her with a smile.

"What of your aspirations, Regina?"

"This is my dream for the future." She blushed and ducked her head. "The school, I mean. Where else can I be myself, doing work I love, dressing how I please, and surrounded by an open-minded community?"

"What of your family?"

"They never knew what to do with me and would be uncomfortable if I lived with them or even close to them.

Thankfully, due to your generosity to your staff and Leah's investment advice, I would not need to live with them again, but I do not enjoy being seen as an embarrassment or never knowing if I have to hide my work, my friends, or my trousers." Regina shrugged. "Once I am too old to run a stable, I'll be a part-time hand with a small apartment or cottage somewhere."

As they were both aware of Leah Godwin's living arrangements, Helen nodded. The retired courtesan was a recruiter and coordinator for the school and spent part of the year in London and part in a boarding house with three other retired courtesans, two of whom were in a committed love relationship.

Like Regina, Helen had come from humble origins. However, she was certain she'd never have gained the independence that Leah, Regina, or any of her instructors had, if she hadn't met and married George by the time she was twenty. It was only in widowhood that she'd found, or been given, the opportunity to forge her own path. The founders of the school were all women except for two earls who were financial benefactors. They had all helped form the curricula and structure, giving her direction on leading its operations.

She'd always hated Society's rigid mores but had managed to remain out of them given her and George's choice of country life. When he had died, she'd been happy to provide a safe place for young women wanting to fight those norms in their own ways. It had felt easy and righteous until Regina touched her. The past fortnight had given her a clearer perspective on the challenges faced by those living outside the rules, and she had only experienced a tiny fraction of what Regina or others had outside these safe walls.

The school remained her first priority, though. Helping the growing number of students who attended each year was her calling. Knowing that someone she cared about saw the institution as their salvation cemented her focus on ensuring its success. If only she could have one day in which she didn't feel like she was one pile of papers away from losing control.

* * * *

Regina stabbed the hay bale with the pitchfork.

"Ouch," Cecilia said.

Regina turned with a questioning frown.

"I was speaking for the hay bale. Has it offended you in some way? You've nearly cleaved it in two, which means twice as many trips into the stall."

Regina grunted.

"Usually, you are grumpy when you haven't had time to ride, but I thought you'd had a nice sojourn today."

She nodded. She had, but it had been a solitary ride—again. Helen hadn't been able to join her for a ride in almost a sennight, and they'd only dined together twice.

The headmistress insisted on having at least one meal a sennight with other staff members to keep up appearances, and she'd had to work through supper two other evenings.

Regina waffled between frustration and fear. Had the headmistress's interest waned? Or had Helen's guilt over breaking her own rules become too much? Helen had made her work ethic clear, so Regina tried to accept her excuses as truth.

None of Regina's prior relationships had been this intense. Their clandestine nature, and the fact that much of the time both parties were simply relieved to find someone who shared their taste for intimacy, meant that she had not spent this much time deepening the emotional bond with a partner. Now, she found her friendship and sexual interest in Helen as intertwined as the knot of broken reins in the tack room. She could pick it apart to try to salvage pieces from it, but it would be painstaking work and not something she relished doing.

All of which meant she'd obsessed over Helen's absence the last two days and now was treating hay bales as though they were potential attackers she needed to skewer.

"Pardon my grumpiness. In fact, why don't you go enjoy your evening with your friends before supper, and I'll get my aggressions out on the rest of the hay? I can finish up, although I always appreciate your help." She managed a smile at Cecilia, though she suspected it was more of a grimace based on the student's stare.

"Better the hay bales than the horses, I suppose." Cecilia tossed her curry brush down on a bench and turned. She lifted her skirts to skip toward the dorm, calling over her shoulder, "Thank you Regina. I hope you feel better tomorrow."

After tackling a few more hay bales and ensuring everyone had food and water, Regina cleaned her apartment. She debated going to the dining hall for a late meal, staying in and scavenging for bread and cheese, or going in search of Helen.

A friend would go check on her, to ensure she was not overworking herself.

Regina snorted, sounding a bit like her equine

neighbors. Her motives were not altruistic, no matter how much she tried to justify her preference. She'd be allaying her own doubts by visiting Helen. Or not.

The stab of fear that accompanied that thought had her on her way to Helen's office. Striding through the dark, she braced for what she'd find. Helen might be poring over paperwork or laughing over wine with another staff member. She might be dismissive or welcoming.

Another shiver of anxiety shook her, and she stumbled to a halt on the path.

Daggers. Regina was in love with her employer. This emotion was supposed to be hearts and flowers. Instead, it ached.

She straightened her shoulders. In for a penny, in for a pound. This surprise visit would either soothe the ache or turn it into a full-blown wound. Either way, she'd carry on as she always did.

My role is secure. That is most important. She repeated the mantra she'd been using all week as her frustration mounted.

She began walking again. Given Helen's concern over the rules, a choice might have to be made. Her position or her relationship. And Regina was no longer certain which she'd choose.

Chapter Eight

Helen looked up at the knock on her open office door.

Regina stood hovering in the portal, her hands twisted in her skirt. Her hair was still covered by a kerchief, telling Helen that she'd come straight from work.

"Hello, love," Helen said, happy to see her lover. Her love. Her heart thumped. Somewhere along the way, she'd fallen in love with this amazing woman. Now she could not imagine a future without Regina. Then her stomach growled, overriding her heart and awakening her to the fact that she'd missed the evening meal again.

Regina remained silent, half in and half out of the room.

"Come in, come in." Helen skirted the desk to take Regina's hand. Tugging her inside, she closed the office door before leaning up to plant a welcoming kiss on her lips. "What a lovely surprise."

"Is it?"

Helen cocked her head, surprised at the gruff question.

"Never mind me." Regina shook her head and waved a hand. "Cecilia told me I was grumpy this afternoon."

"Why?"

"I missed you." Regina lowered her gaze with the

admission, and Helen swore the stablemistress's cheeks colored in embarrassment.

"Well, you have me now, and I am ever so thankful to be had. My head hurts from staring at paperwork for too many hours. Have you eaten?"

Regina shook her head.

"'Tis too late to request a private supper, but I had hoped to grab food and come see you. So let us raid the kitchen. We can nibble in either your room or mine."

Regina nodded.

"Right, then. You are quieter than normal tonight. We shall get sustenance, after which I shall pester you to talk to me. I'd like to help if I am able."

After foraging for bread and cheese, they aimed for the closer room—Helen's. She hastily cleared the small table of papers, poured the wine, and laid out their pickings.

She touched Regina's hand as the other woman reached for the half loaf of bread. "What is amiss, love?"

Regina shook her head, shrugged, then frowned.

"All that then?" Helen teased her.

With a half-smile, Regina admitted, "I didn't like missing you."

Helen's heart panged again. "If 'tis any consolation, I missed you too, you know."

"It is, actually. Not because misery loves company, but I wondered…"

"Out with it. I can only allay your concerns if I know what they are."

"I understand your priority is the school, and you worry about the rules. We talked about you needing a few examples of why this was worth the risk, and I suppose my fears got the best of me. I worried whether you felt you'd sampled enough." One of her shoulders hitched up as she half-stated, half-asked the last part.

"Oh, Regina, love. No. I am sorry. I don't mean to neglect you—"

Regina shook her head adamantly.

"—or even spend less time together. 'Tis just the new program and more staff and more students mean more work. I've deferred more than ever to Grace, but if I run her off by overburdening her, we'll be in even more dire straits. I lose sleep at night worrying about what I haven't gotten to yet."

"I know. I shall likely request two more additions to the stables—horses, not people—in the next quarterly review, given the increase in humans. I was not placing blame. My imagination simply got the better of me. 'Tis apparently dangerous to leave me alone too long. I come up with all sorts of daft ideas."

Helen laughed at her attempt to lighten the mood.

"Thank you for coming to find me. Clearly, we both needed this time more than we realized. Those daytime rides were so helpful to my sanity. I'd return with much-improved focus for the rest of the day. I am frustrated 'tis been so difficult to break away for them."

Regina gave a mock gasp as though affronted, placing her fingertips on her chest. "You're saying the night-time rides aren't helpful? I must work on my technique."

"Ha!" Helen gave a shout of shocked laughter. "They most certainly distract from my focus on work but are helpful to other things than my sanity. *You* are helpful to my well-being."

"Hmm. I think I needed to hear that. Thank you, Helen." Regina leaned across the table to claim her lips in a gentle swipe, tasting of wine and smelling faintly of hay.

Helen sighed through a smile as Regina broke off the kiss. She wanted to shout her love to Regina, but she needed to spend time thinking about how they could progress. Time she wasn't willing to take away from the joy of their new bond.

"Tell me the best and the worst of your tasks. There must be some parts you like," Regina asked.

Helen pursed her lips. "I still love the aspects that were needed from the beginning. The strategizing. New students to be recruited carefully. Instructors who share our beliefs and who are experts in their field must be found. I enjoy vetting sponsors and ensuring they will maintain our confidentiality before approaching them about prospective students. And designing new programs is a delight, although that is generally a group effort."

"What does that leave?" Regina asked, agog.

"Far too much! We have a small team of accountants for incoming and outgoing funds, but I still must keep an eye on the books. And one cannot simply design a program and hand it over. There is space to be found, the appropriate props—" She gestured vaguely in the direction of the newest building, Cheltenham Hall with various businesses and storefronts modeled inside for their mercantile program. "—and detailed curricula to create. Students' grades are reviewed and communicated tactfully to their sponsors, and sponsor visits must be coordinated and supervised."

"Ah." Regina sat back. "You do not like the details, the minutiae."

Helen stared. "I never realized it, but you are right.

'Tis the repetitious work and the tasks to implement the bigger decisions that bore me. I want to move on to the next big thing."

Regina nodded.

"How very aristocratic of me." Helen waved a hand. "I have said it is so. Now make it so."

They both laughed.

Regina sobered. "That is not it, from what I see. Some people can see the larger swaths of strategy, their long-term implications, their selling points. Others easily identify the steps needed to implement those and delight in checking each step off a list. 'Tis about finding the right people for the right tasks. Or in this case, perhaps giving each of the roles to people who enjoy them."

"Right now, we do not have the people. And I cannot seem to find the time to search for and hire them. 'Tis a never-ending circle of frustration."

"I wish I could help. The best I can offer is to stop by at lunchtime if I haven't heard from you and try to pull you away for one of those focus-enhancing rides."

"How about one of those focus-*distracting* rides right now, love?" Helen grinned as she stood and tugged Regina up, stepping into her and wrapping her hands around the taller woman to tangle in her hair.

* * * *

Two mornings later, Regina was ecstatic to find Helen in the stables dressed to ride, although the headmistress stipulated that it needed to be short. After their sojourn, Regina took the reins from Helen as she dismounted, resisting the urge to step closer and allow that lush bottom to slide down her front. Tossing the leather ribbons over the horses' heads, she led their mounts to the stables, passing them to a hand to be rubbed down.

Turning back to thank Helen for the ride, she found the lush bottom already retreating from sight up the path to the main school building.

Ah, well. At least the other night's conversation helped Regina understand the stress Helen was under. Regina recalled that it had also resulted in her being under something else, and smirked. She lingered and enjoyed the view for a moment.

Turning, she saw Cecilia approaching, her gaze flicking between Regina and Helen's retreating form.

"How was your ride, Mistress?"

"Excellent. The weather has held this sennight, and the horses love it."

"And you?"

"I love it, too."

"Hmm."

Regina frowned, wondering if they were still talking about the weather. Best to change the subject. "How are classes?"

"I always enjoy them, but I am struggling with the current topic. We are talking about how to ask for things you like."

Regina's brows rose. She knew much of the topics in the advanced course from bolder students in the past so she understood the reference, but she was surprised at the girl's choice of topic. Cecilia had not discussed any of the classes on intimacy with her to date. "How so?"

"I cannot imagine, if someone is touching me in a private area"—the girl blushed, despite her training to date—"redirecting them. It seems the height of rudeness."

"Hmm." Regina was thankful for her conversations with earlier students. She was no instructor, but she had ways to help Cecilia clarify her understanding.

"What if a man seemed interested in a friend of yours but had not yet asked her to dance? Would you perhaps hint to him that she enjoyed the waltz?"

"Probably. It depends on the man. I wouldn't want anyone to step on her toes."

"So, you'd request a change in behavior on behalf of a friend?"

"I suppose. Yes."

"Now, I know you've learned some of this in earlier classes. What if you were giving someone pleasure in an intimate setting, and if you changed one little thing, their pleasure would be much more intense? 'Tis not to say they aren't enjoying your, um, attentions. I am simply saying if you pinched just so, or flicked your tongue a different way, their eyes would roll back."

Cecilia was blushing, but her hand across her mouth could not hide her grin. Nodding, she replied, "I see your point. I would certainly want them to tell me. Ah, for someone's eyes to roll back for me. Or mine for them. I can only hope I am so lucky when I leave here."

Regina hoped that at the courtesan auction in London, the girl would be chosen by someone who cared about her pleasure as much as his own. Everyone deserved that.

Helen's first explorations of her body flooded her brain, and Regina nearly groaned. The headmistress had proven her leadership skills and not waited for direction. Instead, she'd asked.

Cecilia was watching her. The girl's gaze slid to

where Helen had last been seen. "I'm guessing you've been directed?"

"Psshaw, I am an expert. No one needs to direct me." Regina laughed, giving Cecilia a friendly shove toward the curry brush. "Now get to work."

Once the girl turned away, however, the stablemistress frowned. This isolated campus was like a small village. Everyone knew each other's affairs, and what they didn't know, they guessed. She could not afford to lose this post, delicious leaders who were fast learners or not.

Helen was right. Their relationship needed to remain secret, and they should do better at keeping it so.

The stab of anguish in the vicinity of her heart took her by surprise.

She'd known from the start the affair must have an end date. It wasn't as though they could marry in the nearest church and live happily ever after. However, she was afraid it was too late to avoid being hurt. Her heart was very much engaged.

* * * *

Helen watched Grace's reactions closely when they discussed the work for the coming days. The young woman wore a small frown, and Helen tried to determine whether it was from concern or concentration. She'd caught more winces and hand clenching the past fortnight, and her concern was growing. Everyone was feeling the burden of growth. Whilst expansion was desirable, it remained a problem—another one that she was responsible for solving.

"How are you doing with the written evaluations?"

she asked her assistant. As students completed their coursework, the instructors submitted assessments of their learnings. After a member of the administration reviewed and approved them, they were given to the girls' sponsors when they arrived to collect their charges.

"I am almost finished reading through them," Grace answered. Her frown of concentration smoothed into a smile. "I love hearing about how each student has grown, and how it may align or differ with what they or their sponsor expected when they first came here."

Helen chuckled, remembering her conversation with Regina. Grace was the perfect complement to her skills and preferences. If only they had one or two additional senior administrators to help.

"Right, then. We're at the end of my list. Have I forgotten anything, or is there something you want to add?" Helen asked.

There it was. Grace winced.

Helen sat up straighter, leaning forward.

"I have a few items. Have you approved the groundskeeper's order for fresh gravel to line the drive to the dormitories that we spoke of a sennight ago?"

Helen closed her eyes. "Drat. No. I will find the requisition and send it out tomorrow."

"It shan't be here in time for the end of the current introductory course then, and rain is forecasted."

"I am sorry. I thought the worst of spring rains were behind us."

Students finishing an introductory course needed several days to pack and be picked up by their sponsor, depending on how far they had to travel. The housekeeping staff needed the remainder of the week to finish laundering the linens for the bunks and reset the dormitories before they welcomed students for the next introductory course. The main drive got the most use that week and could quickly become muddy with all the traffic. In addition to carriages getting stuck, which was a bigger challenge than she liked to contemplate in a school staffed entirely of women, people—Regina—could slip and hurt themselves carrying students' trunks to and fro.

She clenched her hands under her desk in frustration at yet another task she'd fallen behind on.

"What about reviewing the proposal for the new advanced class?" Grace questioned. Every instructor was invited to propose a new class. Advanced classes were shorter than mercantile or introductory classes with a wider variety of special skills offered. Even students who had suggestions were encouraged to partner with an instructor so the proposal met academic standards. The latest one had been waiting for her review for a fortnight.

Helen shook her head, wanting to lay it on her desk and weep. Defeated, she wondered why she thought she'd have time for a friendship, much less a romantic relationship. The neglected tasks being voiced felt like punishment for reclaiming her evenings to spend with Regina. Yet, she did not regret any of it. Regina was more important than falling behind in her duties.

Grace was not finished with her chastisements. "Have you received any responses to your inquiries for another assistant?"

"A few. I will follow up on them today or tomorrow, although I don't know where I'll find the time to travel to London." Regina floated to the forefront of Helen's distractions again. Perhaps they could go together. No, that would be too obvious. 'Twas bad enough she was circumventing the rules. Which meant she'd have to go alone and miss more nights with her newfound lover.

A furrow kept appearing between Grace's brows. Her tone was flat when she responded, "We'll ensure everything runs smoothly here when you go, as we always do."

Helen cocked her head. Something was amiss. She dithered on whether to ask her about it or wait for the young woman to come to her when she was ready. Sighing at the list of tasks she already had, Helen decided to let it slide.

Aloud, she added, "There is also a board of overseers meeting in a sennight. I've written to them asking them to find candidates who might be interested."

"What of the recruiters? I know they generally focus on determining fits for prospective students, but perhaps we can ask them to consider instructors also?"

"An excellent idea. Thank you, Grace. I shall write to them today." She scribbled a reminder on her to-do list.

Grace pressed her lips together.

There was definitely something on her assistant's mind, but she often needed time to consider issues before bringing them to Helen's attention. The clock on her desk seemed to tick louder as Helen scanned the list they'd discussed. She could hardly wait to see Regina.

"Have you heard from Miss Jenkins yet?" Grace referred to Beth Jenkins, a former student who had taken almost every class offered before returning to her cousin's home in London. She volunteered with the charity school that had helped found this program and had a knack for matching people's needs. Helen hoped she had a few people who needed roles and would suit both skill-wise as instructors and in outlook with the school's philosophy.

"No, but I'm sure I shall, as we correspond regularly about her husband's goods." Even before they'd been married, Beth had helped Robert Orford create a catalogue for his intimate leather apparel and accessories to sell to and through the school.

Come to think of it, there were some interesting leather dildos in that catalogue. Perhaps a gift for Regina...

She shook her head as Grace rose, collecting her pile of paperwork to return to her office. She was already behind on work. There was no time to dally on gifts for her sexy lover, much as she'd like to.

Chapter Nine

Helen had been doing some research. "I want to see if I can bring you to ecstasy with only my mouth."

They sat at the table in her sitting room. In an effort to see Helen more and avoid more staff knowing the frequency of their evenings together, Regina had begun waiting until the close of the night-time meal hours in the dining room, then request whatever was left from supper to be packaged for her to take away.

Now, Regina blinked and pushed her plate away. "You need only say a few more sentences like that one and you are likely to succeed."

Helen laughed, pleased.

They raced each other into Helen's bedroom, almost trotting with anticipation. Once there, Helen gestured. "Undress for me, please. I am quite sure I could not accomplish that with my mouth."

Regina leaned in for a quick kiss. "You as well."

They both rushed to unlace and peel off layers.

"Lie down, please."

"Shall I tie your hands?" Regina wiggled her brows.

Helen considered it. "Not this time. That might be the intermediate level."

Regina laughed. "Right, then. I have no idea what you have in store for the advanced course. Apparently, you should be teaching some of these classes."

Helen considered Robert Orford's catalogue again.

They needed to peruse it together. That would have to be here in her suite of rooms. It would be hard to justify carrying it down to the stables, should she be seen.

Leaning over her lover, Helen braced herself on her hands and knees, starting with a long kiss before dragging her lips over Regina's biceps and up to her shoulders. She moved above her, brushing her breasts against Regina's, allowing them to sway side to side an extra time or two.

"Hmm. I thought you said only your mouth. If it didn't feel quite so good, I might say this is cheating."

Helen nipped her rounded shoulder muscle then trailed her lips down Regina's chest, giving her breasts attention. Her mound heated and grew wet. While part of her wanted to rub herself against Regina as she explored, a bigger part was interested in completing this challenge.

Her hair brushed Regina's chest as she lowered to lick the taut stomach muscles under silky smooth feminine skin she so enjoyed. Skipping Regina's center, she tongued her knee, then sank her teeth gently into her strong thigh muscle before nudging her legs apart with her chin.

"Mistress, you are amazing. If this is an introductory level experience, then you get exemplary marks."

Helen snickered. "You haven't even gotten an orgasm yet. You're too easy a grader."

"Right, then. Let's see what you've got."

Helen nodded, and on the upswing, swiped her tongue hard and fast up Regina's core.

Regina nearly shot off the bed. "Daggers. That was intense."

Helen settled in, squirming a bit between those long, toned legs. "Hold on for the ride."

Nudging Regina's lips apart with her nose, she licked and sucked, paying attention to when the prone woman's breathing caught. When it did, she repeated the motion, narrowing her focus and roughening bit by bit as Regina liked.

Finally, she buried her face in her folds, pressing with her mouth and nose as she firmed her tongue and thrust it over and over.

"Ah, ah. Love," Regina panted, barely able to form words. "Put yourself over my leg."

Helen realized she'd been grinding herself against the bedcover to no avail and happily swung her leg over Regina's. Rounding her back, her core hit Regina's shin. Regina had widened the splay of her legs so she could still put her mouth where she had pledged to. But now, she could also rub her most sensitive flesh to her own orgasm simultaneously.

Returning to lap at Regina, she could see her clitoris fully exposed and swollen and teased it with her tongue for a few seconds, finding the right angle for her own friction.

"Please, Mistress."

Helen pressed her face against Regina, turning her nose back and forth, tonguing her channel and grinding herself down on her lover's shin until they exploded together.

As they snuggled together, Helen's head in the crook of Regina's arm, the stablemistress smiled against her hair. "First in class."

* * * *

Today is going to be one of those days.

Helen had overslept, thanks to their snuggling leading to another round of sex that delayed sleep by several hours. And an introductory course finished today, which meant none of her other work got done. Instead, she'd spend the next two days meeting with sponsors who wished to discuss their students' progress. In between, she'd send each of the departing students off with a hug and encouraging word.

On top of that, it was raining, which meant the staff had to work extra hard to keep the steps and halls from being slippery. Lugging the students' trunks to their carriages across mud would only add to the staff's overwork. She regretted again not having gotten around to ordering more gravel in for the drive to the dormitories. The staff's struggles were her fault.

It was not even lunchtime, but Helen had only had time for one cup of tea and no food before the madness began. She was hungry, tired, and irritable, yet she was expected to be warm and welcoming to the demanding sponsors. Helen was ready to beg for five minutes to herself so she could at least gulp another cup of tea. Days like this made loving her work harder.

Another carriage rolled up, the sponsor alighting to bow over her hand with thanks. Helen leaned sideways to look inside the carriage to ensure he'd brought a maid as chaperone. His fiancée, Katherine, had been given her family's permission to attend the school on condition that all proprieties were maintained.

Katherine came down the stairs at a jog, her face alight at seeing her betrothed. Halfway down, her booted foot slid on the wet stone. Only with Helen's and the gentleman's quick steps forward to catch her hands did she avoid a fall.

Regina appeared around the corner with the girl's smallest trunk.

"What are you doing with that?" Helen snapped. The stress of the day and her concern turned her voice sharp. Katherine's near miss made her picture the stablemistress slipping and falling as she'd done weeks ago.

Regina started, nearly dropping the trunk. Looking at Helen curiously, the taller woman handed the trunk off to the carriage driver to tie down.

"The last thing we need is for you to fall today." Helen's waspish tone shocked even herself. She stared at Regina in mute apology.

"Right. Better the twenty-five-year-olds with half my strength fall under the weight of the luggage." Regina growled and stomped away.

"Damnation." Helen whispered under her breath as Katherine's carriage rolled away. Yet another thing wrong she'd have to fix.

* * * *

Regina really needed to stop clomping around, the horses were giving her the side-eye. But every time she recalled Helen snapping at her, an angry pulse beat at her temples and her jaw clenched.

The headmistress had never interfered in Regina's duties before, or her choices when she opted to help on the busiest move-in and move-out days.

She has no right to tell me what I should and shouldn't do. Especially as by night, she waxes poetic about my muscles in between running her tongue over them.

Cecilia stumbled into the stable, winded. She shook rain out of her hair then wiped her face. Holding out a note, she gasped, "Mrs. Montague asked me to deliver this as soon as possible."

"Did you run all the way here?"

"Yes. She seemed…upset. I don't think I've ever seen her agitated before. And, well, you two…" Cecilia trailed off uncertainly.

And she yelled at me for walking *in the rain.*

Unwilling to see where Cecilia would take that statement or respond to her unspoken question, Regina simply said, "Thank you for delivering this. Please be more careful on that path, though. You saw what happened to me."

Cecilia nodded and waved as she left.

Unfolding the note, Regina scanned it.

R~
I will come and apologize in person tonight, but this is my start: I am very sorry. I was (am) tired and hungry and…no matter, 'tis no excuse. Whilst it was not well done of me, my question came from concern for you. What can I do to make it up to you?
~H

Regina's reread that last line and began to panic. What if Cecilia read the note? But Helen would not have given it to someone she did not trust, and the headmistress had as much to lose as she did.

Folding the missive, she slid it into her bodice to keep close to her heart. Five minutes later, she rolled her eyes and retreated to her room to tuck the paper under her smallclothes in her top dresser drawer. She couldn't even manage to be romantic. Now her left breast had a papercut, and she'd spilled water on herself trying to be careful to not splash the letter.

For the rest of the day, she remained in the stables, helping expedite the students' departure as best she could from there. She readied students' horses, helped coachmen turn in the muddy yard, and kept the trough under the stable's overhang full of food and water for the carriage beasts.

As she worked, she stewed. Cecilia was right, she'd never seen the headmistress in a state other than serene, at least in public. She smirked at memories of Helen's non-serene states at times in bed. Shaking her head to clear it of the daydream, she returned to the problem at hand.

Helen would no doubt be harder on herself than anyone else, even with Regina being the injured party. She was already anxious about the expansion of her duties as the school grew in size and scope. This momentary lapse in professionalism would only worsen a stressful day.

Perhaps she should have sent a note back with Cecilia or even later in the day. But she wasn't sure what she could say. The lines between personal and work relationships had been blurred, and Helen was her superior. She was at a loss.

She kept reminding herself she was living her dream, no matter what happened with Helen. However, her chest hurt the entire afternoon, albeit not from the stupid papercut. This felt much more like heartache.

Chapter Ten

Despite the longer hours of daylight, it was dark by the time Helen finished ticking names off her graduate list and checking on the housekeeping staff regarding their turnover of the introductory class dormitory.

Grabbing a cold meat pie—she'd apologize to the kitchen tomorrow—and a decanter of wine, she picked her way down the muddy path carefully. It wouldn't do to fall after yelling at Regina for tromping about. Besides, she was so exhausted she needed to be extra cautious.

She'd managed two more cups of tea and a pastry on the run, but she was ravenous. Sniffing the meat pie in its muslin wrapping, she almost hoped Regina had eaten. Helen shook her head—she was clearly delirious. She didn't even know if Regina would allow her entry.

Regina was pacing the wide center hall of the stables, muttering at her equine friends as they poked their heads over the stall doors. As Helen's skirts swished into hearing, she turned.

"Hello, love. Have you eaten?" Helen asked once she'd neared. She tried to keep her voice even and easy, but inside, she worried about her welcome. Her hands were damp from nerves, and she clutched the wine tighter.

"No," Regina flicked her gaze down, then back to Helen's and grinned. "I also brought snacks from the kitchen in case you hadn't eaten. We shall have a feast."

"Excellent, I've barely eaten all day. My apologies will be more coherent with a few bites of food in me, if that is permitted?" She did not want to presume even the smallest thing after her actions earlier. A small part of her was surprised she hadn't been yelled at yet. She deserved to be.

Regina caught her arm in one hand and the wine in her other, pulling her forward. "Of course. Let's get you fed."

After inhaling a quarter of the meat pie in three bites, Helen sipped her wine and sat up, feeling much more coherent and ready to beg for forgiveness. "I am sure I don't need to tell you how full move-out days are. And as you know, I awoke late and did not have time for breakfast. I was tense and hungry, then I saw you and pictured you slipping and simply snapped." Her words poured out in a rush. "There's no excuse for my tone, no matter what the circumstances. I humbly beg your pardon. Whilst it came from concern, 'twas not well executed."

"I understand." Regina had leaned forward to listen to her explanation, her eyes steady on Helen.

"I am happy to make it—" a huge yawn escaped "—up to you." Thankful Regina seemed to accept her plea, Helen propped her elbow on the table and her head on her hand to stare at her beautiful lover, a silly smile lighting her face. If only she could find the energy to stand, she'd drag Regina to bed and apologize properly. She'd been contemplating various alternatives all day.

"You are forgiven. No need for acts of contrition." Regina sounded almost amused as she moved their plates aside.

"You're sure? I had an excellent plan." Helen's words slurred with exhaustion. It was all she could do to stay awake.

Regina must have noticed. "Perhaps tomorrow night then. Come to bed. 'Tis late, and you're exhausted. I shall rub your back, and I promise to wake you earlier tomorrow."

Stripping to their chemises, the women brushed out their hair and braided it before crawling into Regina's narrow bed.

Helen curled on her side, half asleep as soon as her head touched the pillow. Regina's mix of soft breasts and gentle hands in counterpoint to her muscular arms and legs surrounded Helen. These were not the actions of someone in a steamy short-lived affair. Helen felt loved and cared for, and she relaxed.

Before the taller woman could even circle her palm once around Helen's spine, her thoughts spun into black silence, and she slept.

* * * *

The next day dawned gray but dry. True to her word, Regina nudged Helen awake with soft kisses before anyone other than the kitchen staff was up and about.

Regina lounged in bed and watched Helen dress quickly, the headmistress not bothering with her hair until she returned to her rooms to change to a new dress. She stood as Helen stepped toward the bed and drew her into an embrace.

The shorter woman ran her hands from Regina's shoulders to bottom, snuggling into her, and Regina returned the caress.

"Thank you." The words were muffled against her throat.

"Try to eat something this morning, yes?" She gave Helen a gentle squeeze before releasing her.

"I shall. Today will be another day of insanity. Perhaps you can come up and bring supper to my rooms later?"

"If you'd like. If you need a night to catch up on sleep without sharing your bed, I understand."

"No. I sleep better with you."

Warmth burst in Regina's chest that had nothing to do with the kiss Helen stretched up to plant on her lips. She'd forgive this woman anything if she could keep her.

Daggers. That risky feeling had never been in her plans or her dreams.

"I must go. I'll see you tonight?" Helen asked as she turned toward the door.

"Certainly." Regina followed her to the door, assessing first the luscious derriere retreating from view, then the weather.

As the clouds remained intact, not releasing any rain, Regina decided it was safe to resume carrying luggage for the students scheduled to depart that day.

Dropping a trunk on the stairs of the main building, she pivoted to return to the stables. Her name being called made her turn.

Grace descended toward her, her face a careful blank.

"Hullo, Grace. How are you faring?"

"I'm exhausted. Who do you think has to cover Helen's tasks while she is indulging in her little infatuation with you?" The words were stilted, said through a clenched jaw.

Shocked, Regina took a breath before replying. Perhaps she had misunderstood. Helen's assistant had been professional and kind throughout her tenure at the school. Helen would not have stood any less. "I beg your pardon?"

"As well you should. Helen and I could hardly keep up with the workload. Then you distracted her, and we are drowning. Worse, she doesn't seem to care. Her focus is whether it's supper time so she can see you."

"Have you spoken to her about this?" Regina asked in a neutral tone.

"I have repeatedly asked her about her progress in hiring another assistant. But nay, 'tis another task that has fallen by the wayside." Grace's hands were fisted at her sides, although she was heedful not to raise her voice. "I am done with taking the brunt of the workload to make her look good. I love this school as much as she does, and I've labored tirelessly alongside her to get it where it is today. I have so many ideas for the future, but no time to implement them. A word of warning—I've written to the board to ask their help in solving this."

Regina gasped. "You didn't!"

"I did. I plan to tell them about Helen violating the school's rules with your relationship and ask that they consider offering me a promotion."

"But-but-" Regina didn't know where to begin. "The only promotion would be Helen's role."

Grace shrugged one shoulder. "At this point, I cannot worry about that, just as she has not worried about me handling the work she unloaded onto my desk." She tilted her head. "If it's any consolation, I think Helen has done enough for the school she'll keep her position, or *a* role here, at least. She owns the land, after all. *You*, however, need to go. As long as you are a distraction, this will continue. And you violated the rules despite knowing them. For heaven's sake, Helen liked men before you started this."

The words stabbed into Regina's heart. Panic flowed through her like a horse stomping on her chest.

The little termagant in front of her did not care about promises between lovers. She'd taken it over their heads.

Desperate, Regina begged, "Please, do not do this. I shall ensure she spends less time with me. No time with me. I will turn her away until she stops coming. I'll stay out of sight in the stables, just as it was before."

Grace frowned. She started to shake her head.

"You have no proof we did anything wrong," Regina said in a rush. "We supped together and talked, as colleagues and friends do."

"Fine." Grace snapped, and Regina sighed in relief. "I shan't raise my *suspicions* of a relationship with them if you cease disrupting Helen's work and this school's future. Unless—"

Regina tensed again.

"—they specifically ask about distractions."

Regina deflated. Of course, Grace would not lie for them. She only hoped it would not come to that. Now she had to figure out how to save both Helen's position and her own by lying to the woman she loved.

* * * *

Placing one last document in her completed pile, Helen stood and stretched.

Through the open doorway, Grace looked up. "Are you leaving?"

Registering the faint censure in her assistant's voice, Helen responded, "I was planning on it. Was there something urgent you need before I go?"

"No." The younger woman gestured to the piles littering her desk. "I have a lot to do before I feel I've accomplished enough to call it a night."

Helen raised her brows but let the jibe pass. "Good luck. I am starving. I do hope you'll get supper before the kitchen closes."

Stepping out, she considered her assistant's response. The end of another day of move-outs was not the right time to have a sensitive discussion, however. They were both too tired and frazzled.

Opening the door to her suite, Helen stepped over the threshold. Paper crinkled under her shoe. She frowned and picked up the folded note to read.

Dear Helen,
I hope your workday went smoothly. I am unable to join you for the evening. It seems people have begun to notice our association and speculate on the nature of it. We'd be best served by pausing or even stopping our activities, as I would never want to jeopardize your dream for this amazing institution you have built. I wish you all the best in the upcoming board meeting and beyond.
Love,
Regina

Helen fell back against the doorframe, sadness taking the strength from her limbs. Her arms dropped, the note crumpling again against her skirt. Her head thunked against the wooden door.

Helen wracked her brain for what—or who—could have brought on this sudden reversal. When they'd spoken of the risks earlier in the relationship, Helen had been more concerned about discovery than Regina. Now, Regina was writing notes and avoiding her for fear of exposure. Something had changed, but she had no idea what.

She recalled Grace's recent strangeness. Could the two be related?

Helen shook her head. There were rarely interactions between the stablemistress and her assistant, and certainly the move-outs the past few days would not have left time for much conversation.

Helen debated returning to her office and getting more work done, especially given Grace's concerns. Perhaps she could make a few gentle inquiries about the young woman's frustrated state.

No. The more pressing issue was the woman she loved. And how could Regina have signed "Love" on such a terrible note? That alone required a conversation. Helen wasn't headmistress of a growing school because she let things go. Stomping out, she beelined for the stables, determined to get to the bottom of this sudden reversal.

* * * *

Regina huddled in the chair farthest from the door to her room. She wanted to guzzle wine and reach for oblivion, but she could never bring herself to lose that much control. Besides, her role as stablemistress did not allow for hangovers. The animals still needed care and were big enough to cause injury if she was listless.

Hoping against hope no knock would sound at the door, no irate headmistress would appear with questions on her lips, she cowered.

When the inevitable knock came, she sighed.

"Regina?" Helen's voice was faint through the wood.

She had a wild thought of hiding and not answering, but that would only delay the inevitable. Placing a hand on the table, she levered to her feet and trudged over to open the door.

"Helen." Her voice was flat.

"What is the meaning of this?" Helen brandished the note.

"You are the more intelligent of us. I am sure you understand."

"I never thought so until I got this. How can such a lovely, smart woman write such drivel?"

Regina's spine went rigid. She'd expected this and was prepared. No matter that she agreed, she had to appear outraged. Helen's position and her own depended on her generally woeful acting ability. "'Twasn't drivel when *you* voiced the same fears."

Helen reached for her, but Regina took a long step back.

The headmistress's face fell, tears welling in her beautiful eyes. "Please, we can be more careful. Perhaps fewer meals. Perhaps more time out here, away from others in the main building. Tell me what you need."

"I need—" Regina sucked in a deep breath. She could do this. Her heart was rending with each word, but she could manage the next few minutes. She'd figure out the rest later. "—you to go."

Helen started crying in earnest, both hands at her

face, the crumpled paper caught in her hair. "You signed it—" Hiccup. "'love.' If you meant it, don't do this. Please."

Regina clenched her hands, every muscle in her body straining toward this strong, intelligent, lovely woman who was hurting, to soothe her, hold her, reassure her. To take that horrible note and shred it and make love to the person she was sure was the love of her life.

Instead, she stood silent and still.

Catching her breath on a sob, Helen scanned her from head to toe and back again. Nodding once, she calmed another degree. "This isn't the end. I will return another time to discuss it further. In the meantime, know this. I love you. I am in love with you. I am not giving up."

Regina bit her lip to hold in her own sobs as Helen nodded again and let herself out. Only when the footsteps had faded from hearing did she throw herself on her bed and bawl.

Chapter Eleven

Helen dragged herself into her office the next morning. Alternate hours of crying and exhausted slumber had not left her well-rested.

Grace, already at her desk, glanced up, then did a double take as Helen passed.

"Helen? Are you unwell?"

Does a broken heart qualify? I do not think 'tis a medical condition. More of an overall life condition.

Aloud, she answered, "A little under the weather, but I shall recover."

Perhaps if she said it enough, she'd believe it.

As Grace's gaze returned to her desk, Helen swore she caught a glimpse of a half-smile, but it was gone in a flash.

"Shall I call for tea, then? When it arrives, I can come in and go through the highest priority items for the day," Grace asked with her eyes and hands still on her paperwork.

"Yes, please."

Helen dropped like a stone into her desk chair. She did not want to be here today.

She could not recall the last time she had thought that, if ever. But if not here, then where? The last place she wished to be was back in her lonely, cold bed with nothing to do but remember Regina's presence there.

I would rather be at the stables learning to muck out

a stall if it meant being with Regina.

Tears sprang forth yet again as she reminded herself that was no longer an option. Dabbing at them with a handkerchief, she attempted to compose herself.

Grace shouldered the door farther ajar and set a tea tray on the sideboard.

"Helen? Are you crying? What is amiss?"

Helen was wary about saying too much, even to her most trusted employee. Her views on qualities of a leader were too ingrained—lead by example—to allow her to admit to having broken the school's rules. "You know Regina and I have grown close, yes? We had a falling out. She does not believe 'tis appropriate for us to spend so much time together." *Or any.*

"Hmm," Grace murmured as she poured and passed Helen's teacup.

Helen's gaze cut to hers.

"If I may say so," Grace said, "it might be for the best. The school needs its leader to give her undivided attention to keep this magnificent institution running smoothly."

Helen cocked her head. That was a strange statement, with a hidden criticism but no names mentioned. "Do you not think it has been running smoothly?"

"I did not say that." Grace glanced down at her lap, smoothing her skirt. Putting her tea aside, she picked up her notebook. "Shall we go over what needs to be done? My list is quite lengthy."

Helen allowed the subject change. Her wounds were too fresh and her brain too sluggish to allow her to follow the nuances of Grace's behavior.

Perhaps tomorrow.

The mail arrived that afternoon. They sent a messenger into the village once a sennight rather than paying the penny post rates, instead paying for their mail at the village's post office. But Helen could not face a new pile of paperwork to sift through, even to hand some of them to Grace. Given her assistant's attitude, she preferred to open them before delegating to search for fraught issues.

So after another restless night, Helen peered at the wax seals and where possible, the return addresses. Most were from sponsors arranging future classes or thanking her for completed ones after spending more time with their family member who had attended. Sometimes they also received notes from alumnae; those were Helen's favorites. While she could have used the encouragement, none were present in that week's correspondence. The current stack included a few from board members, likely requesting additional topics for the board meeting in a few days' time or confirming their attendance.

Beginning with these, Helen smiled when she saw Leah Godwin's name on a return address. Leah had met Helen's sister, Teresa, through the charity school in London and in turn helped the founders set up the School of Enlightenment. Not only was Leah a recruiter for the school and member of the board of overseers, she was a friend.

Helen started to read eagerly, hoping Leah might be planning to stay an additional day or two so they could catch up after all the board business had been completed. The letter was not about that, however. She slowed her reading, then began at the top again.

Scarcely able to believe Leah's words, she sat back, staring at the door in shock. After long moments, she gathered herself, ready to confront her accuser.

"Grace?" she called.

Her assistant poked her head in. "Yes?"

"I need you in here for a minute, please. And close the door."

The young woman's brows rose, but she complied, grabbing a pen and notepad before settling in a visitor's chair.

Helen handed her the letter. "Care to explain this?"

* * * *

Grace read through the letter then set it down and straightened in her chair, her back not touching the wooden slats. "I love this school, and I want the best for it."

"And you think I am no longer the best." Helen was furious, not at Grace's opinion, but at the fact she hadn't come to her to try to resolve any issues.

"You have been distracted. Even trying to hire another assistant has been delayed, which might have helped."

"Why not approach me and have a frank discussion?" She was trying to understand, even as her hands clenched in her lap, and her pulse raced.

"I kept asking you about tasks, including hiring, to no avail. If we cannot keep up with the current workload, how could I raise the new ideas I have? I refuse to see my hard work and others' be wasted because the school fails whilst you engage in a tawdry liaison—one which is against the rules!" Grace's voice rose with each word until she was almost shouting.

"You could have outlined your suggestions the

same way all staff are invited to do about new class topics and other ideas." Helen's words came through gritted teeth in an effort not to match Grace's volume. "We teach independence and responsibility here. And we teach adults, not children who go tattling to others. If you felt I was not fulfilling my duties, you should have come to me. This"—she grabbed the letter and waved it—"is immature and unprofessional."

"I did try." Grace's mouth pulled tight, her tone sullen. She could not meet Helen's gaze, however, and her focus remained on her lap.

"Not enough. Asking about individual tasks is one thing. Intimating to my superiors that I am shirking my responsibilities is quite another. You knew how this would look." Her tone pensive, she added, "Perhaps you hoped they would put you in my role. An affair against the rules gives you the perfect reason."

Grace flinched but did not deny it.

"You could have come to me with that, also." Helen let the silence linger when Grace did not respond. She was sad as well as angry at the lack of trust from her assistant, and those emotions were obscuring her usually clear vision of solving a new problem.

"Now what?" Grace echoed her thought, glancing up then back down.

She shook her head. "I don't know. I need time to consider this. But know this. If I ever hear you refer to my relationship with Regina as a tawdry liaison again, our working association will be at an end."

Grace's head jerked back.

"You have no idea what is between Regina and I. And whilst it is none of your concern, I shall share this: I am in love with her. The biggest slice of my anger is my belief that you hurt her by warning her away from me."

Grace swallowed. "Helen, I-I had no idea."

"I'd advise you to make yourself scarce the rest of the day. I will send a note to your suite when I have studied the situation and am ready to move forward."

"Yes, ma'am. Helen—"

"I don't want to hear another word right now. Any further conversation I could manage would not be productive or professional."

* * * *

Regina alternated stomping and moping when she was alone with the horses. When others came to ride or help, she attempted normalcy. In both situations, she reminded herself this position was her dream, as was Helen's role, and she'd made the right choice. Opportunities like this were beyond rare. She could find another woman.

But she'd never find another woman like Helen.

Most helpers came and went without noticing anything amiss, but Cecilia had spent more time with her. They were at the water trough filling buckets, and Cecilia kept shooting her side glances.

"Mistress," came in a near-whisper. "I noticed you haven't been as happy the past few days."

"Hmph. If one does not have less joyful days, then how does one appreciate the really great ones?"

"That is very philosophical. Rumor in the main building is that Mrs. Montague has stopped her staff suppers recently. Might that be the reason for your less happy days?"

Regina shot her a look. "What have I told you about gossip?"

"You enjoy hearing it but won't contribute to it?" Cecilia asked with a grin and a wink.

The stablemistress snorted, sounding much like one of her charges.

"I've noticed Mrs. Montague has darker circles under her eyes than normal, too," Cecilia offered with a small shrug.

Regina's glance was sidelong. She tried not to encourage, but she was dying for information on Helen.

"And no one knows anything about it, but Grace carried her work down the hall to a meeting room yesterday. Do you think they had a tiff?"

Regina stared at her directly now, alarmed. "Has that ever happened before?"

"Not that I know of, and I asked a few staff members in the main house."

If only she could check on Helen, even as a friend. But the risks of being seen were too high, even with Grace out of sight.

"You'd best get to class, missy. Enough gossip with the beasties and their mistress."

Long after Cecilia had left, Regina questioned why Grace would have moved down the hall.

Shaking her head, she got back to work. Helen could fight her own battles if Regina eliminated the risk of a rule-breaking romance. She needed to stay out of the way.

But it felt wrong. And was this really her dream post now? Or would any horses and any situation do if she didn't have Helen in her life? Given the choice, she'd take Helen and dealing with miserable misogynistic men any day.

She chuckled at her ridiculous alliteration. *I'll have to tell Helen. She'll get a good laugh from that.*

Then her brain caught up to her heart and tears sprang to her eyes as she brushed the last mare. She'd never cried this much in her life. She was glad Cecelia wasn't still there.

Cecilia. Helen. This role. Regina's mind raced. She had told Cecilia if someone had information that would help her please them more, she'd want to know it. The same would go for protecting themselves from attack, professional or physical. She'd been so caught up in worrying for her own employment, but knowing Helen was more important than her position made everything suddenly crystal clear.

To hell with her future here. She needed to warn Helen.

Daggers. Classes had finished for the day. If she was seen in the main building, rumors would fly again, and Grace might hear them.

In the morning, after another sleepless night wondering if Helen would believe her or if she'd even see her, Regina dressed with more care than most days and strode up to the headmistress's office.

To no avail. The outer door to Grace's office was closed, with a sign pinned to it saying "Board meeting preparation in progress. Please see one of the instructors if you need assistance."

* * * *

After a day and a half covering the must-dos of daily management for the school while debating her approach,

Helen had a plan.

Grace had worked elsewhere the day before, and while Helen worried the girl was still scheming, she thought it equally likely the assistant was writing to other schools to try to secure a position. Either way, she'd been grateful for the peace and the time to strategize.

That first morning, she'd flipped through the piles of work in front of her, noting with regret some had sat longer than she'd ever allowed before. She considered whether Grace was correct.

Perhaps.

It did not justify Grace's behavior, and Helen *had* been attempting to remedy the situation by hiring another assistant. However, they were still falling behind.

So how could she fix the situation?

Regina's observation that she preferred the strategic aspects to her role over the tactical had resonated. She'd believed with another assistant she could narrow her duties to strategy and client relations. But ultimate responsibility for this ever-growing school would still sit on her desk as headmistress.

Her first reaction during the argument with Grace kept bouncing around in her head. *I do not want to be here today. I would rather be at the stables learning to muck out a stall if it meant being with Regina.*

She was still passionate about the success of the school. However, she was more passionately in love with Regina. She needed to do right by them both.

Grace's passion for the school was still growing. Admittedly, the girl had gone about it the wrong way, but that was because her strength was in tactics, not strategy.

Helen sketched overviews of various solutions.

Names and arrows of reporting responsibilities littered several pages. She drew empty boxes where they'd need more staff. Once she had one she believed would work, she was ready to tackle her next conversation with Grace. Then she—or they, depending on how the discussion went—would fill in the responsibilities for each role.

She'd sent a note to Grace to clear her calendar for the day and be at Helen's office bright and early.

Grace walked in with a tea tray, which Helen took as a tacit apology and a good sign. A silent nod was her greeting, after which she put her notebook and pen to one side and poured and passed Helen's tea to her, settling in her usual visitor's chair.

"Good morning, Grace. Thank you for the tea." Helen was determined to start politely and formally and judge how the meeting would go based on Grace's reaction.

"You are welcome. How…can I assist you?"

"I spent yesterday preparing a plan for the board meeting."

"A plan? Had they requested such an item?"

"No, but I ardently believe in this school and its continued success and growth. Therefore, I believe we have reached a point where we need a new plan."

Grace's mouth twitched toward a prideful smile.

"I thought long and hard about what you said—your accusations." Helen frowned and her tone firmed to ensure her assistant recognized the error of her ways.

Grace flinched, her expression flattening. She stared at Helen warily.

"Whatever degree of accuracy you had, you went about change in the wrong way."

"I know." Grace nodded, ducking her head for a

moment. "I see that now."

"Good. Because I need your help with the details of this plan." Helen nudged two roughly drawn organization charts toward her. "My enthusiasm and my willingness to direct all energies into this institution may or may not have dimmed. They may simply not be enough given the school's growth. You, however, are younger and your passions run high. I believe between the two of us, with appropriate help, we can make this school the best it can be."

Grace peered at the two pages. "What are these?"

"The first," Helen tapped it. "Is what I am proposing on a trial basis. Your role would change from being an assistant *to* the headmistress to becoming an assistant headmistress. We would each have our own assistants, to be hired, but you would remain reporting to me."

"Oh?" Grace's gaze flew to hers, and her back straightened from leaning over the document. "Helen—"

"Note I said trial basis." Helen wasn't finished. "What you did broke our trust, Grace. You will need to rebuild it over the next few semesters. However, I find I no longer want to work as hard as the breadth of these programs require, so changes must be made. This gives you the chance to prove yourself worthy of being a leader of this school. Which leads me to a potential future state." Helen tapped the second paper.

It showed a headmistress and a provost. Anywhere else they might be considered the same role, but her intention was different.

Grace tilted her head as she studied it.

"My vision is to have the headmistress be the client-facing leader, dealing with sponsors, recruiters, prospective students. The work you know I love, and I know you don't. The provost in the meantime would deal with the daily operations of the school. The work you love, and I do not." She gave a small shudder at the mere thought. "Both would report to the board and interact with them, and they would need to work closely together. Trust would have to be absolute."

"Helen—" Grace seemed to be grappling for words. She took a moment to press trembling fingers against her lips. "Why would you do this after what I did to you?"

Helen raised her brows.

"I mean, thank you. Thank you! It all sounds heavenly. But…why? I was so sure I deserved this or more when I wrote to the Board, but now, I believe I have so much to learn from you, the first being how to handle difficult conversations."

Helen snorted, and Grace responded with a wan smile, still waiting for her answer.

"A truly great leader must recognize when they have reached the limits of their time, acumen, or desire. However painful it was to hear, your criticism made me realize I had reached at least one of mine. This school runs in my blood, and I will never abandon it. But I am ready for a new phase of my life. I never expected a second chance at love. Now I've found it, I must make time for it. Besides which, an infusion of young blood and new ideas—tempered by partnership with age and wisdom—can only help students."

Grace was now crying.

"There is one last stipulation, though," Helen warned.

Her assistant looked up through her tears. "The board must approve?"

Helen waved a hand. "I doubt they'll have an issue if we request this together."

"What, then?"

"An apology to Regina. And…"

Grace grimaced.

"She must sign off on the trial period before the role of provost is instated. Words are cheap, and your actions hurt her as well as me."

The younger woman nodded in acknowledgement. "I know. And truly, I am sorry for all of it."

"All?" Helen arched a brow.

"Well," Grace drawled with a small smile. "Perhaps not the result, but how I went about everything."

Helen nodded at the clarification before outlining the day's work. They needed to list out responsibilities under each role in both scenarios. Helen could hardly wait for the board meeting to finish so she could share all this with Regina and build the next stage of their lives together.

Chapter Twelve

Regina had left a note under Helen's door asking her to come to the stables but received no response. With only one day left to the board meeting and overseers arriving throughout the day, Regina left another note describing Grace's threat and warning Helen so she would not be surprised in the meeting.

Silence reigned. She wondered if Helen believed her or if she could not fathom her beloved assistant turning on her. She'd been up to the main building twice, despite the risks, but the outer office door was shut with the same sign.

She rode almost every mare the school owned on the first day of the board meeting in an effort not to burst in and warn them of Grace's duplicity. It would counter the purpose of such an interruption, giving away their relationship by the act itself.

Exhausted, she collapsed at her little table at the end of the day with a glass of wine. Sipping it, she waited. She'd bide her time until well after supper and take her chances and knock on Helen's door.

When sharp raps sounded at her door, Regina jerked in surprise, nearly spilling her wine.

Twisting the knob, she flung the door wide, wanting all human interactions to be done for the night.

Helen stood there grinning.

"Wha—?"

"Oh, good. You have wine." Helen bustled by her, wearing a fancier dress in a deep purple and a more elaborate hairstyle than she usually did. There was a bounce in her step as she aimed for the little corner table.

"Helen. Please, come in. Would you like…I see you would." She shook her head with a smile as Helen took a gulp from her glass before glancing around for the carafe and a second one. "May I ask why you're here?"

"You needn't ask. I shall tell you." Helen snickered at her own silliness. She was clearly in high spirits. "The board meeting went well today."

"It did?" Regina asked. Concern about the following day's portion of the meeting warred with hope. "Did you get my notes?"

"Yes, thank you. I am very sorry I did not reply, but we were working day and night to get our plan fully outlined to present to them. And I wanted it approved before I showed it to you."

"To me?" She could not fathom a reason she'd need to see a school plan.

"Yes. Come, sit. Have some wine." Helen seemed unable to stop smiling.

Bemused by Helen's words and her gaiety, Regina went over and sat as Helen pulled two pieces of paper out of her pocket.

"Leah Godwin wrote to me to warn me about Grace's actions. I confronted Grace, and she was quite critical, saying I was distracted and had let things get away from me."

Regina growled.

"I was a little. By the most beautiful diversion I could imagine," Helen said, patting her hand. "But more, the reality is that even with hiring another assistant, the school needs more leadership. I was an impediment."

"You keep saying 'was,'" Regina interjected, suddenly worried despite Helen's cheerfulness.

"I love this school too much to continue to hinder its progress, once I recognized the issue." Helen pushed the pages toward Regina. "These are what I proposed."

Regina tried to make sense of the lines and words on the page, but her thoughts were circling about what she'd do if Helen left. She couldn't bear this place without Helen. Perhaps the headmistress could pursue a role she loved and, if amenable, Regina could go with her. Would Helen want that? Regina could only hope.

After a long moment, the words and lines came into focus, but still did not make sense. Pushing them back, Regina shook her head and asked, "I am sorry. Can you explain it to me please?"

"Running a secret, growing school requires passion. You pointed out that only certain aspects of my work excited me. I carved those out and will keep those." Helen pointed to a cluster of words with an arrow to the word "headmistress" in a box. Pointing to other boxes and arrows, she continued, "Grace will report to me but take on more responsibility, and we'll both have assistants to share the work. If she proves herself, then we will lead the school together, both reporting directly to the board."

This turn of events was unanticipated, but with each sentence, Regina's concerns grew. "Why would you do such a thing for someone who betrayed you? She does not deserve your generosity."

"Perhaps." Helen shrugged. "That is why she has to prove herself. The board was not impressed with her methods, either. I had to insist."

"But why? And how do you insist to your superiors?"

"Because her actions show she has the passion required for this school. And I insisted by informing them I had broken the rules and intended to continue to do so. Thus, they'd need to find a way to ensure those rules did not apply to my position."

Petrified by all the ways that conversation could have gone wrong and terrified to hope, Regina clutched her hands in her lap and stared, mute, at the love of her life.

"I love you," Helen said.

At first, Regina assumed she'd imagined the words or perhaps said them aloud. But Helen looked at her expectantly.

"Regina, I meant what I said the other night. I am in love with you. Forging a life with you is my new obsession. I will always want to be a part of this school, but not to the exclusion of being able to be in a loving partnership in the open."

Silent tears of joy and relief rolled down Regina's face before she covered it with both hands.

"Hey now, please don't cry. You shall make me cry." Helen reached for her hands, peeling them away from her face to squeeze them.

"You asked me about my dream situation, and I said here. But this was yours, too. It feels as though you are giving up too much. For what? For me? That feels wrong. I'm just a stablemistress."

"No. You are so much more. Do not belittle yourself. Do you love me?" Helen asked, her voice suddenly timid.

"Yes! I love you so much." Regina squeezed

Helen's hands. "I was half in love with you after a month of working here. I was not sure I could bear working here without being with you, but Grace—"

"Ah, yes," Helen interrupted with a start. "I neglected to finish describing my plan. There is another condition of the new roles." Helen outlined the requirements between Grace and Regina.

Regina grinned at her through her tears. "You are devious."

"Why, thank you."

"Helen. I can scarcely believe this. Are you sure?"

"Absolutely."

"No one has ever chosen me first. 'Tis a little hard to take in."

"Likewise, no one has ever supported me like you have. Even with George, I was the supporter, as I did not have a career. This is a unique and wonderful partnership for me, as I said."

"So, what now?" Hope burgeoned in Regina's heart for a wide variety of possible futures with Helen by her side.

Of course, Helen had a plan for that as well, which Regina thoroughly enjoyed.

* * * *

Helen hurried along the path to the stables, excited to be done with her work for the day and to see her love.

It had taken almost two months of long hours and several trips to London and beyond to find the right fit for an assistant. Grace had taken equally as long, but they were finally fully staffed. Then it had been another month of training the new women in their roles.

Thankfully, one was an alumna of the school and was able to help the other.

Grace had been quick to acknowledge at the recent quarterly board meeting that roles were still being defined and she was not yet ready to step up to co-lead. Helen had been impressed but not surprised. She'd known Grace's over-aggressive approach had stemmed from eagerness rather than viciousness, and as it had gotten Helen what she wanted most, she was inclined to forgive the transgression.

Regina, however, was going to be a bigger challenge. Grace recognized that, and Helen suspected that was where Grace's willingness to defer the last step in organizational change came from. However, the two had forged an uneasy alliance after Grace's initial apology and were edging toward more cordial terms.

As she turned through the doorway of the stables, she was surprised to find Grace chatting to Regina.

"Good evening."

"Hullo, love." Regina tugged her closer and planted a quick kiss on her lips, and Helen melted.

Grace watched them with a smile.

"Grace, were you looking for me?"

"No, actually. I had been to the village. When I returned the mare I borrowed, I saw a note to both you and Regina, so I gave it to her."

"I'll have you know my desk is much saner these days," Helen said with mock outrage.

Regina snickered under her breath, and Helen elbowed her.

"It is, it is," Grace answered, hands out in supplication. "I simply saw her first."

"Hmph."

"If you are very nice, I shall read it to you," Regina teased. "'Tis from Leah."

Helen grinned at them both. Their lighthearted banter eased her worries another degree. Also, she and Grace both were done with work for the day while there was still light in the sky, which was a good sign for the future.

"Come on, love. Let us swing by the cottage and see how the construction is going." Regina tugged her hand. She kept her room at the back of the stables for the time being, Helen kept her rooms in the main building, and they alternated. Regina was still getting accustomed to the idea of not being within hearing distance if any of the horses were upset. Nevertheless, they were framing a cottage a short way off the path between the main school and the stables, where Helen and Regina would reside. Helen had received pre-approval from the board but was financing it with her own money. Because the land was hers until her passing, they were willing to grant her leeway. She'd taken advantage of that fact and ensured they'd allow Regina to remain there should Helen predecease her.

They strolled hand in hand toward the pile of stones and half-finished walls. The cottage had enough of a frame that the roof was completed, so they no longer needed to worry about rain delaying the project.

Regina stepped over the empty threshold and held her hand out for Helen. They stood hip to hip, arms around each other, looking at the half-built interior.

As she did every night, Helen put her head on Regina's shoulder and said, "I can't wait."

And as she responded each time, Regina answered, "I can. The only essential in my life is in my arms."

Want to read more about the School of Enlightenment?

Get a free prequel to the series when you sign up for Maggie's newsletter here:
https://BookHip.com/DRDDJCW

~*~

Keep reading for an excerpt of
Roslynn's Rebellion

SOPHIA'S SCHOOLING

An innocent country girl...a jaded earl...an education in pleasure.

Orphaned at eighteen, Sophia has learned love means loss. Now she must leave her country home to navigate the opulence of the London Season, although she has no desire for romance or a husband.

Edward, the newest Earl of Peterborough, is struggling with the business of his family estate. He has shunned marriage due to a shameful secret, but with his title comes the need for heirs.

Despite their misgivings, Sophia and Edward cannot resist their attraction. When she accidentally discovers his penchant for spankings, her curiosity is her undoing. A clandestine meeting risks a scandal. Only marriage to a reluctant bridegroom can save her reputation. But perhaps the School of Enlightenment can give her an education in love.

PENELOPE'S PASSION

Schooled in the art of pleasure, her real passion is baking. Required to marry, the earl's heir finds his new courtesan more to his taste.

After her mother's death, Penelope Wood's hope of opening a bakery falls victim to the real need to support herself. When four retired courtesans present her with a temporary yet lucrative path back to her dream, she wants to hear more. Attending the School of Enlightenment, participating in a Virgin Auction, and becoming a courtesan all sound feasible. The most important rule--do not fall in love.

Lord Michael Slade, heir to the Earl of Mansfield, loves his family above all else, cooks for relaxation, and revels in his membership to a discreet spanking club. But his father is ill, and his mother is pushing him to marry. Even so, when he meets a dark-haired beauty who doesn't mind a good spanking and discovers she's up for auction, he can't let her go to another man. He has to have her...at least until he finds a wife.

With an inevitable marriage looming and a vow to remain faithful to his hypothetical bride once he's engaged, both Penelope and Michael must protect their hearts, even as they find a connection they cannot deny.

ALTHEA'S AWAKENING

A widow with no knowledge of carnal desire, a rake bored with even the most hedonistic pleasures, and a game of truth or dare...

Lady Althea Egerton's late husband secured her independence when he left her his apothecary. After two years of growth, she is ready to expand the business...if she only had capital. Finding a wealthy husband would solve that problem, but Althea refuses to subjugate herself to another man. She prefers an investor.

Unfortunately, the only one she knows is the golden god of hedonism, and his help comes with a price.

Evan Gardner, Earl of Cheltenham, is bored. At twenty-eight, he has no equal in business, politics, or seduction. None of them hold his interest. Even his annual week-long orgy disguised as a house party leaves him cold. Yet the prudish widow, who wants only his money, intrigues him. As neither of them wants the trappings of marriage, a dalliance with the elegant widow might be just the challenge he's been searching for.

Though Althea cannot resist the lure of ecstasy he offers as condition for his assistance, a continued liaison could risk her reputation and her store's profits. To win this negotiation, Evan will have to ensure she can have both independence and pleasure.

BETH'S BEHAVIOR

An outrageous free spirit meets her match in an introvert with a secret leather business

Raised as a free spirit, Beth Jenkins refuses to submit to the Ton's rigid rules. She has fun where she wants, with whomever she wishes. By day, she excels at matching people's needs with those who can provide them. That talent and her cousin, Lady Althea Egerton, are the only barriers standing between her and complete ostracization.

When her cousin requires an investor for her business, Beth gains them an entrée to a house party hosted by a wealthy earl, where she encounters Robert Orford. The intimate leather apparel and toys of pleasure he creates entice Beth as much as the man himself, and she is determined to pursue him.

As the stocky second son of an earl, Robert was bullied as a child and hates being in the public eye. Beth's behavior is far too outrageous for his tastes. If only she didn't have the curvy figure he most admires, perfect for testing his leather pieces.

But Beth refuses to be tamed, so if she can't convince him to care less about society's disapproval, they could be forced to walk away from the perfect partnership for leather and love.

ANN'S ANGEL: A Regency Christmas short story

December 1812—London
Two courtesans looking to get out of the game...

Ann Dockree wants this Christmas to be her last as a courtesan, but learning that her latest investment did not return the expected funds crushes her. Especially since her dearest friend Mary Hale has enough saved to quit the life and leave London.

But when, only days before Christmas, Mary is hurt at the hands of her so-called benefactor, Ann must care for her. Touching Mary is its own sweet agony, torturing Ann with fantasies of what might be. If only Ann can summon the courage to confess she wants more than friendship with Mary before it is too late.

A warm bath, a compassionate touch, and an unexpected yet longed for taste of pleasure might inspire the Christmas gift that offers happiness to both.

Excerpt from **Roslynn's Rebellion**

Chapter One

Lady Roslynn St. Pierre shifted on her dressing table stool as her maid finished fussing with her hair.

When her mother knocked and entered, she used the excuse to stand. Her coiffure was good enough. She had more important things to consider this evening.

"Mama, how do I look?"

"You are always beautiful, my dear, but tonight you are absolutely radiant."

Ros had chosen a burnt sienna ball gown to complement the chestnut locks finally piled on her head in pin-tucked curls. Lady Nicole, Countess of Effingham, wore a darker, shimmering rust gown, to accent her similar-colored hair that showed slivers of silver.

"Given the possible importance of tonight," her mother continued. "I thought you might like to borrow my pearls?"

Ros's brows rose in surprise as she noticed the necklace her mother held toward her.

Mama's pearls? She must really want the Earl of Suffolk as a son-in-law. Who wouldn't, after all? The man is delicious. That blonde hair flopping over blue eyes, those shoulders…

A tremor ran the length of her spine as she conjured his image. Beyond his appearance, she'd been intrigued by her father's stories of the brash young man who had stepped into Parliament as the next Lord Suffolk after the previous earl's passing.

After a particularly late night in Lords then White's, her mother had asked her father about his evening as Ros joined them at the breakfast table. "Suffolk—the new Suffolk—is full of opinions, and they aren't always popular with the old guard."

"On what, Papa?" Ros asked.

"Rather a lot, poppet, but he seems most passionate about fair laws that affect the working class. I shall keep my eye on him. We have needed a champion for some bills, and he is quite eloquent, despite his lack of experience."

Then they'd been introduced at a ball, and his startling azure eyes and fair hair ensnared her attention. When he called on her two days after their first dance, their conversation about his focus in Parliament and hers at the charity school wove the web ever tighter. She'd hoped he felt the same—a partnership between them would be magnificent.

He'd singled her out for dances at several recent balls and called on her after each. If he requested a dance again tonight, it would be tantamount to announcing a formal courtship.

As Lady Nicole fastened the pearls around her daughter's neck, Ros raised a hand to caress them. "Thank you, Mama. Let's hope they work."

Her mother had worn that necklace the night the Earl of Effingham had asked for her hand in marriage, and she'd told Roslynn that since then she'd worn them whenever she needed a little extra luck.

"I see no reason why they wouldn't. Suffolk is

clearly interested in you. I have no doubt that if he attends, you'll get another dance and mayhap even a request to court you." She smoothed a wayward curl off Roslynn's cheek.

"'Tis not as though I have accepted other invitations. After the second time he called on me at home, the other men stopped."

"Your dance card remains full, however. He needn't know that others aren't calling upon you. 'Tis a good thing to promote competition. You are a valuable commodity, and he needs to stake his claim or step back."

Ros snorted. "You make me sound like a piece of property."

"Negotiations of marriage contracts and those for property are not so dissimilar, my darling." Her mother shrugged stoically and stepped back to run a critical eye over her daughter.

I don't want to be a commodity. I want him to be as enamored of me as I am of him. Please let this be more than an infatuation. I hope for a partnership like my parents have.

"Will Teresa be there?"

"Yes, and Beatrice."

"Hmph." Her mother's opinion of Beatrice was mixed and evident in her grunted response. Ros and her two closest friends volunteered at a charity school for orphaned girls. Their passion for the work kept Beatrice in the countess's good graces.

Both friends had married last Season, which also provided a modicum of stability. That change also fueled Roslynn's readiness to find her one and only—Teresa and Beatrice had both married for love.

"I am glad they'll be watching out for you. I know you dislike when I hover too closely."

"I appreciate your concern, Mama." Ros laid a hand on the matronly arm that fidgeted with a fold of her skirt. "I shall be fine. Even if Lord Suffolk does not come through. You've taught me to take care of myself."

And if he does, I shall consider exactly how I'll look out for myself.

* * * *

After a round of dancing, in which she'd had the pleasure of Lord Suffolk's shoulders for a waltz, Ros took a break to sit with Teresa and Beatrice along the ballroom wall.

She leaned in, her voice low but excited. "I received word today that Katherine was accepted to the governess position she wanted."

"Excellent," said Teresa, Countess of Carlisle, from the farthest chair. "Well done, Ros."

Katherine, at eighteen, had recently graduated from the charity school. More than work in the classrooms, the women's greatest zeal was to find girls suitable placements which provided stability.

"Yes, well done. But right now, I want to dance. Where is my husband?"

Teresa rolled her eyes. "Oh, Beatrice. He only walked away to get you a lemonade, you besotted fool."

"Yes, yes, I am." Beatrice, now the Countess of Shaftesbury, grinned. "Ohh, speaking of besotted fools. Look who is coming this way!" She clutched Roslynn's arm.

They watched the Earl of Suffolk approach. He was

delicious in his blue jacket, gold waistcoat, and buff breeches. His blonde hair, too fine to curl in the latest fashion, swept over his forehead. His focus was trained on Roslynn.

"We danced already this evening. Oh! Do you think...?" Roslynn's smile was almost as big as Beatrice's had been. She hadn't considered the possibility of this development.

"He hasn't even declared a formal courtship. To leap to dancing with me twice will set the tongues wagging." Ros laid her other hand over Beatrice's in shock.

The Ton had an unwritten rule—if a gentleman danced with a lady twice in an evening after courting her, he effectively declared his intention to request her hand in marriage.

"Yes, indeed I do." Beatrice's nod was emphatic, her fine golden hair shaking in its pins.

Roslynn sucked in a breath. "Oh, my."

"Decide now," Teresa whispered out of the corner of her mouth. "If you don't want that—him, we shall all retreat to the ladies' retiring room."

Ros appreciated her friend's offer, but she'd already made her decision. "Thank you, but no. I want him."

Beatrice bounced once with glee. "Of course you do."

Teresa nodded at her, ignoring the other woman. "Right, then. Have fun." She sat back, smoothing her skirt, her gaze narrowed on the gentleman striding toward them.

Lord Suffolk arrived and made his bow. "I am surprised to see three such lovely young ladies sitting. I expected you to be surrounded by bucks requesting a dance, or on the dance floor."

Beatrice fanned herself. "I agree. Which is why I am about to find my husband." She nudged Teresa.

"What? Oh, right. I suppose I should as well. My own husband, that is."

Everyone grinned. The ladies stood and shook their skirts out with a rustle before accepting the earl's bow and separating to locate their spouses.

"Lady Roslynn, I believe I can remedy this situation for you. Would you be so kind as to give me another dance?" He held out his hand.

"Why, yes, my lord. I should like that." Placing her gloved hand in his, Roslynn rose. Her cheeks were warm and her fingers trembled, knowing the magnitude of her acceptance. But she wanted this. More than a partnership, she saw the possibility of feeling about him the way Beatrice did about her husband.

Love. This second dance meant she really needed to look out for her own interests…tonight, before things went further.

As they circled the room, she noticed heads leaning toward each other to point out this second dance. Her nerves got the best of her, and she gasped for breath as her heart pounded. This might be her last dance as an unattached débutante.

Worse, what if it was not?

"Lord Suffolk, might we take some air on the veranda?"

His eyebrows rose, and his gaze ran over her flushed countenance.

"Of course. Please." He twirled her out of the rotating dancers and walked her over to the doors. It was drizzling, but as in most London homes, the veranda was covered.

"Better?" he inquired, peering at her.

"Yes, thank you." She looked down as she felt her cheeks heat. Her etiquette training had not covered how to handle a proposal. All the ballrooms and flirting had not prepared her for a private conversation with such a handsome, eligible earl. On top of which, she was about to ignore all rules of propriety.

Given the coolness and the rain, only a few other guests were present, and she wandered toward the opposite end of the veranda, hoping he'd follow.

"Lord Suffolk—"

"Nicholas, please."

Hmm. That would not be appropriate, at least for the time being. On the other hand, she was contemplating kissing him…

"Very well, when we are alone, Nicholas." She compromised, then hesitated. She wasn't sure what she wanted to say—what she *could* say—without being seen as forward.

"Lady Roslynn—"

"I think 'twould only be fair to offer you the use of my first name, as you have done the same." She smiled at him.

He returned the smile and began again. "Roslynn, I have had the privilege and honor of making your acquaintance these past sennights. I hold you in the highest esteem. Dare I hope you feel the same?"

"Yes."

"Yes, I may dare? Or yes, you do?" he asked with a wink.

Her laugh tinkled out, and she glanced around to ensure no one was paying them any mind. She had ulterior motives, after all.

“Both.” She grinned, gaining courage. This was her opportunity.

“Phew.” He gave an exaggerated wipe of his brow. “Excellent. Then, I should very much like to—”

“Kiss me? Yes, you may dare that as well.” She gave a decisive nod. Inappropriate or not, Lady Roslynn St. Pierre very much intended to ensure that her future husband kissed well before she committed to anything.

* * * *

Nick stared down at this most gorgeous of creatures, a woman he desperately wanted to be his bride. He’d chosen her because she was the epitome of decorum. She performed charitable work. She presented herself in the latest fashion while remaining modest. She could talk to anyone about almost anything. Indeed, she was the belle of the ball again tonight, at least in his view. And would make a strategic partner for his efforts in the House of Lords, in addition to maintaining his various homes and creating beautiful children.

What more could any man want? Especially one who had spent the last few years trying to remove any stain of rumor from his name.

A request for a kiss. Then his conscience kicked that answer away. *That is* not *the height of decorum. ’Tis a warning sign.*

She still watched him, eyes narrowed at his delay.

She was right. Whatever his scruples had to say, he *wanted* to kiss her. And she had managed to give him both the means—an invitation—and the opportunity, there in a dark corner of a deserted veranda.

He grinned, his hands moving to grip her arms above her elbows, where they bent to clasp her hands in front of her. "Excellent. You are most gracious with your affections."

Her eyes widened.

In surprise? With nerves? She had invited him. He was merely accepting. He leaned in, pulling her arms toward him at the same time.

She took a small step closer, knuckles pressing against his waistband.

Besides her luxurious reddish-brown locks, her fair complexion and lustrous brown eyes that seemed lit from a fire within, he loved her height. She was mayhap four inches shorter than his a-hair-under-six-foot frame. Quite reachable for a kiss, and for all sorts of…

Hmm, best not to think of that just now. At the moment, he was grateful for that height. If she'd been shorter, her hands would have hit a rather shocking bulge at his groin when he pulled her to him.

Aanndd, that thought does not help allay the bulge.

He moved his hands to cup her head carefully so as not to muss her updo, and tilted his head to bring his lips to hers.

She gasped in his mouth.

He took advantage, his tongue sweeping in. He felt her jolt of shock but did not release her. Rather, he pushed his frame into her hands, wanting to touch as much of her as he could. Teasing her with flicks of his tongue, alternating with soft twists of his lips against hers, he reveled in her lemonade-tinted taste, her roses and vanilla sweet scent, the warmth of her breasts and belly a breath away from his.

Feeling her hands move, he exulted. They slid

around his back to clutch at his jacket, and he obliged her unspoken request, nudging forward those last scant inches to press against her, chest to breasts, belly to belly and—*damn me, that's delicious*—pelvis to pelvis.

Nick had a sudden fear of his cock's demands to get through the clothing and to her hot center and almost wrenched away. They were on a veranda at a ball, for heaven's sake. Knowing she did not understand the effect of the kiss on him, he withdrew his tongue, then lips, slowly, gently. He raised his head but lingered when he saw her lust-glazed eyes, swollen glossy lips still parted as though inviting him back, and flushed cheeks. Her breasts plumped up further over her gown's neckline from being pressed against him. He bit back a groan.

"Roslynn. I had this all planned. My reasons, my hopes. I shall discuss them with you tomorrow, I promise. But for now…it is my sincere hope…I would like—" He stopped and took a deep breath. "Please do me the honor of becoming my wife."

She sucked in a breath and her eyes held a new sheen. Her voice was a thread when she gulped and replied, "Yes, please, Nicholas."

"I shall call on your father tomorrow."

* * * *

Roslynn hovered in the front parlor from the moment she woke the next morning. She brought her notes on the new school she and her friends had been discussing, her needlework, and a book. None kept her interest for long. She vacillated between bouts of attempted productivity and pacing by the window, far enough back, she hoped, that she would not be noticeable to anyone approaching the front door.

Hours later, after she had declined lunch, Nicholas's horse approached. He dismounted and she admired his muscular bottom. *I must find an opportunity to squeeze that.* As he handed the horse off to a groom and mounted the few stairs, the tight breeches strained over thigh muscles built from riding, making her groan.

Uncertain if he'd greet her or approach her father first, she bounced in place, wringing her hands in a jumble of nerves and anticipation. Then, when no knock sounded on the parlor door, she paced again. She'd already assured her father she welcomed Nick's suit, so she expected it would be quick, but time slowed to a crawl until she heard her father's office door open again.

Too impatient to wait, she walked to the hall door and opened it. She stepped out as the older earl and Nick started toward her. Her father nodded once to her and drew back, and Nick came forward alone, his broad shoulders obscuring her father's retreat to his sanctum.

He reached for her hand and bowed over it, his lips brushing the back and sending a shiver up her spine.

"Come in, please. Would you care for tea?"

"Thank you, but no."

"How did your conversation go with my father?" They settled in chairs angled together, with the door open as a nod to etiquette.

"We've reached an agreement; he will write the contract and send it over. But Roslynn, I want to ensure you are happy with this arrangement. To that end, I should like to discuss a few things now, and I'll review the contract with you when I receive it, if your father hasn't already done so."

"Thank you. 'Tis quite unusual, is it not? Why

would you do that?" Ros's breath hitched, her pulse fluttering in surprise. While such a thing was unheard of in the Ton, she was pleased he'd offer that consideration. Still, it was important to understand her potential husband's thinking.

Nick leaned forward, reaching for her hands. "For the same reason I asked for your hand. I desire a partner. You must know something of this from our conversations about Parliament and my goals. I need someone to support my bids for allies. You are a social creature. I am not. And your reputation is above reproach. While I work in Parliament, you can work in the Ton if you're willing. Unlike so many of the Marriage Mart misses I've met, you and I have discussed enough to know that we share ideals. You are too intelligent to be my social secretary and housekeeper. I want more. Hence the idea of a partnership."

"Oh, Lord Suffolk—Nicholas. Yes. That sounds wonderful. More than I dreamed. Thank you." She squeezed his hands as her infatuation took a step closer to the cliff of falling in love.

"Right, then. I wanted to ensure you understood and shared my vision. Now, do you have any questions for me? Any concerns?" He gulped and glanced away before returning his gaze to hers.

Roslynn frowned in confusion. Had her father brought up Nicholas's past, despite her insistence she didn't care? Why would she have concerns? She'd already agreed, last night and this morning again. He was peering at her closely, seemingly watching for any reluctance. She hastened to reassure him. "No, my lord. I am quite happy." One side of her mouth quirked up as she pressed her advantage. "Well, mayhap one question."

"What is it? Anything, my dear."

Her voice went to a breathy whisper. "Another kiss, please?"

His eyes widened and he barked the start of a laugh, quickly forming it into a cough so no one would check on them.

"In your father's house? I think not, Roslynn. Your reputation is above reproach, and I would hate to ruin it before I even make you mine." His voice was sterner than she liked, but she acquiesced. For the moment.

"Very well. I shall ensure we take a long walk in the garden on your next visit." She winked at him.

Acknowledgments

I got the original idea for this story as part of HEA Collective's second season thanks to Kelly Cain, author of fabulous contemporary romances.

Special thanks to my editor, Diana Carlile, and my friend Cecilia Rene who writes Regency romance, for allowing me to honor them by using their names.

Always, my real-life romance hero, my husband, gets the biggest thanks of all.

About the Author

Maggie Sims began her love affair with romance before her teen years, drawn to the Regency by her mum's British influence. In her twenties, she did her best to live the Carrie Bradshaw life in New York City, albeit with less expensive shoes and more books.

Despite reading hundreds of romance novels in her life, she was still blown away when she met the love of her life, an ex-Marine cinnamon roll with creative woodworking and culinary skills.

Having retired from corporate life, they live in Central Texas and are parents to a varying number of dogs and cats. When not writing, Maggie is a wine enthusiast, a travel junkie, and a romance reading fiend. She also sporadically crochets for KnotsofLove.org and does just enough exercise for that second glass of wine at night.

To find out more about Maggie's latest reads, favorite wines, and travel destinations, sign up for her newsletter.

~*~

Contact Maggie at
www.MaggieSims.com

www.ingramcontent.com/pod-product-compliance
Lightning Source LLC
Chambersburg PA
CBHW072138300726
48975CB00003B/1114

* 9 7 9 8 8 9 0 4 4 4 0 3 5 *